THE MAYFAIR MISTLETOE PLOT

TRACY GRANT

O Romeo, Romeo, wherefore art thou Romeo?
  Deny thy father and refuse thy name.
  Or if thou wilt not, be but sworn my love
  And I'll no longer be a Capulet.
  —Shakespeare, *Romeo & Juliet,* Act II, scene ii

DRAMATIS PERSONAE

*indicates real historical figures

<u>The Rannoch Family & Household</u>

Mélanie Suzanne Rannoch, playwright and former French intelligence agent
Malcolm Rannoch, her husband, MP and former British intelligence agent
Colin Rannoch, their son
Jessica Rannoch, their daughter
Berowne, their cat

Laura O'Roarke, Colin and Jessica's former governess, teacher, and writer
Raoul O'Roarke, her husband, Mélanie's former spymaster, and Malcolm's father
Lady Emily Fitzwalter, Laura's daughter from her first marriage
Clara O'Roarke, Laura and Raoul's daughter

Alexander (Sandy) Trenor, Malcolm's secretary

Elizabeth (Bet) Simcox, his wife

The Davenport Family & Household

Lady Cordelia Davenport, classicist
Colonel Harry Davenport, her husband, classicist, former British intelligence agent
Livia Davenport, their daughter
Drusilla Davenport, their daughter

Edith Simmons, classicist and former governess

Archibald (Archie) Davenport, Harry's uncle, MP, and former French intelligence agent
Lady Frances Davenport, his wife, Malcolm's aunt
Chloe Dacre-Hammond, Frances's daughter from her first marriage
Francesca Davenport, Frances and Archie's daughter
Philip Davenport, Frances and Archie's son

The Mallinson Family

Arthur (Julien St. Juste) Mallinson, Earl Carfax, former agent for hire
Katelina (Kitty) Velasquez Mallinson, Countess Carfax, his wife, former British and Spanish intelligence agent
Leo Ashford, her son
Timothy Ashford, her son
Guenevere (Genny) Ashford, Kitty and Julien's daughter

Hubert Mallinson, spymaster, Julien's uncle
Amelia Mallinson, his wife
Lucinda Mallinson, their youngest daughter

David Mallinson, MP, Hubert and Amelia's son
Simon Tanner, playwright, his lover
Teddy Craven, their ward
George Craven, their ward
Amy Craven, their ward
Jamie Craven, their ward

Others

Thomas Thornsby, classicist

Marianne Schofield, his fiancée
Gerald (Gerry Schofield), her brother, classicist
Sophia (Sophy) Schofield, her sister
Sally Schofield, her sister
Billy Schofield, her brother
Theodore Schofield, her father

Charlotte Wilcox, Marianne's best friend

Justine Lambton, Gerry's friend, classicist

Lady Shroppington, Elsinore League member, Thomas's great-aunt

*Emily, Countess Cowper, patroness of Almack's

CHAPTER 1

Mayfair, London
December 1820

"You needn't look at me as though I'm going to break. It's hardly a surprise."

Cordelia Davenport set down her copy of the *Morning Chronicle*. Edith Simmons had lived in the Davenport household for almost a year. She helped look after Cordelia's children. She was no stranger to Cordelia's own tangled history. But Edith remained very self-contained in many ways. For all they had been through—three murder investigations, blackmail, multiple spy plots—Cordelia had rarely seen Edith visibly shaken. And she'd certainly never seen her cry. "Did you know?" Cordelia asked.

"Thomas mentioned it when I saw him at the Classicists' Society on Monday."

Two days. Cordelia had been at the Classicists' Society lecture on Monday as well. She and Edith had walked home together. And Edith hadn't even been red-eyed. "It must be—"

Edith straightened her shoulders, fingers steady on the book she was holding. "Thomas and I've known for ages that we couldn't marry—if we ever even thought it was a possibility. We've known he needed to marry an heiress to have any hope of helping his family. It was inevitable really. So the fact that he's actually betrothed shouldn't come as a surprise."

"Shouldn't isn't at all the same as doesn't." Cordelia had very vivid memories of her own response when the man she had wanted to marry had become betrothed to an heiress. She scanned Edith's face. Edith's hazel eyes were steady, her pointed chin set with the usual determination, her strongly marked brows vivid against her pale skin. Though she might be self-contained, Edith had never really tried to keep her feelings about Thomas secret. They spilled out, the way her red-brown hair constantly escaped its pins.

"All right." Edith threw the book in her lap onto the sofa beside her. "I knew marriage was impossible for us. I wasn't even sure I wanted to marry if we could. I told myself domesticity was a trap and I was fortunate I couldn't be caught in it. But no matter how much I knew, how much I told myself, this brings home that it really *is* impossible. And that's absolutely beastly."

"Thank goodness." Cordelia jumped up from her writing desk, ran across the sitting room, and dropped down on the sofa beside Edith. "I was afraid I'd completely misread you. Or that you weren't human."

"Oh, I'm all too human where Thomas is concerned." Edith slumped back against the green-and-white-striped sofa cushions. "She has a younger brother, Gerald, who's come to some Classicists' Society talks. He's at Cambridge still. I think that's how Thomas met her, though he didn't volunteer a lot. Do you know her? Marianne Schofield?" Edith's voice caught just the slightest bit, like the toe of a half-boot scraping on rock, as she said the name of Thomas Thornsby's betrothed. Words could have power, as Cordelia's writer friends would be quick to concede.

"I know the family a bit," Cordelia said. "Marianne was a child before Waterloo and then we were in Brussels and Paris, and since we've been back in London we haven't gone about in society as much as we used to."

"That's because you're sensible," Edith said.

"That's a matter of perspective, I suppose. I prefer our life now." Cordelia scoured her memory of Debrett's and other social details. Though she might be more focused on classical studies and nursery and schoolroom activities and the occasional murder investigation or spy mission these days, recalling those details was still second nature. "Her father did very well betting on a British win after Waterloo. Which one can hardly fault him for."

"Her father made his money in munitions. He supplied cannon and guns to the army during the war in the Peninsula."

"So I've heard. Her mother is connected to the Gorings. Lord Pemberton is a cousin, I think."

"So her father married into the fringes of the beau monde. And he wants more for his daughter."

"It's the way things are often done," Cordelia said. "It's a trade that's worked for generations. One of my ancestors was the daughter of a wealthy brewer in the time of Henry VIII who married a penniless baron. And then their son became a viscount. So one could say the bargain worked. But how well the marriage works rather depends on the expectations of those involved."

"I imagine Thomas is clear-eyed." Edith grabbed a pillow and hugged it to her chest. "He's a pragmatist. But he also takes his commitments seriously. He'll do his best. Though if she wants town dash she'll be disappointed. And I can't imagine she's—I doubt she's a classicist. If she were, you'd think she'd have come to the Classicists' Society with her brother."

"Yes, precisely. I doubt it as well. And it's difficult to see Thomas with anyone who isn't a classicist."

Edith shrugged. "Lots of people in Mayfair marriages keep to their own pursuits. Didn't you and Harry at first?"

Cordelia grimaced. Her gaze went to her writing desk, which

held notes of a monograph she was writing with Harry. And to the two toy horses occupying a makeshift stable beneath the desk. "With a vengeance. Though even then we talked about classics. In fact, those were some of our best conversations. We spent our wedding journey tramping about Yorkshire looking for potsherds. At the time I was simply grateful to have something we could do together and something to talk about at dinner. Looking back, I was happier then than I'd been in months. Years. Not since—" But even now, even with Edith, who knew so much, she wasn't prepared to talk about George Chase. His life and death and the way she had felt about a man who had been capable of so much perfidy still rubbed her raw. Instead, she said, "It was classics that gave Harry and me a basis to make our marriage work, though I didn't realize it until years later."

Edith plucked at the fringe on the cushion. "People make marriages work without having things in common though. I don't think Thomas expects—That is—"

"I'm quite sure he doesn't," Cordelia said.

Edith stretched her legs out and frowned at the toes of her half-boots, dusty from her recent expedition to Green Park with Cordelia and her daughters. "I hear she's very lovely. One of the season's successes."

"She's pretty," Cordelia conceded. "Far more conventional than you." Edith might not be the type to be crowned the toast of the season, but to Cordelia's mind she was the sort one would never forget. "Though she appears to be far less silly than a lot of young women who are just out. Oh, dear, that makes me sound ancient."

Edith folded her arms, crushing the pillow. "I expect she'll make Thomas an admirable wife."

Cordelia glanced down at her wedding ring. And then at a diamond bracelet Harry had given her. Which perhaps meant more. "Define 'admirable wife.'"

"Oh, you know. The sort who knows how and when to pay

calls and what to order for dinner and how to seat a table and arrange flowers—all the things you know how to do."

Cordelia felt her spine jerk straight. "Edith, do you really think me as dull as that?"

Edith's gaze shot sideways to Cordelia's face, at once level and abashed. "Of course not. But you can't deny you know how to do it all."

"Only because I was brought up to it. No, that's not fair—you were too."

"I just didn't pay attention."

"And I used to think it was important. But Harry doesn't care a rap for it. In fact, he'd much prefer it if we went out even less than we do. I don't think Thomas does much either."

"No, but he'd notice if his house weren't the way it's supposed to be," Edith said. "Perhaps more than Harry would. While I'd be perfectly comfortable with the chaos. I suppose that doesn't give a lot of thought to any possible children."

"Oh, children do fine with chaos," Cordelia said. "I raised mine through Waterloo and the aftermath and then through abruptly packing up for Italy. As long as they have their parents and basic comforts of life, they seem fine. It was rather a relief to realize that."

The door opened to admit Harry. He hesitated on the threshold, as though aware he'd interrupted a personal discussion. For all his brusque manners, Harry was extraordinarily attuned to personal nuances.

Cordelia stretched out her arm to him over the sofa back. "I'm glad you're here, darling. Did you see Malcolm?"

"Yes." Harry moved into the room. "Malcolm and Mélanie have invited us to dinner tonight. Kitty and Julien will be there." His gaze moved to Edith. Just the barest flicker.

"How splendid," Edith said. She looked from Harry to Cordelia. "Truly. I mean, it's going to be a bit ghastly facing everyone with the news of Thomas's engagement out, but I'll have to do it sooner or later. They'll all be kind and they won't pry. And truly I could do with distraction tonight. If only there were a good murder investigation or a set of stolen papers or a bit of political blackmail to be resolved that I could help with."

Harry's face relaxed into a smile. "Careful what you wish for."

Edith grinned. "Honestly, right now any of those sounds like heaven."

MÉLANIE RANNOCH POURED a cup of coffee and passed it to Edith Simmons. Edith was doing splendidly, all things considered, accepting everyone's sympathy (largely unspoken, for it was a tactful group) and not giving signs of feeling sorry for herself. Mélanie, who had had a varied romantic career in her years as a spy, had never been in the position of having a man she loved become betrothed to someone else. Though she certainly had wondered often enough if her husband Malcolm would have been happier with someone else. She caught Malcolm's gaze across the sofa table. Malcolm smiled, an easy smile that said he had no hint of the doubts that still ate at her.

Edith took a sip of coffee and settled back on the library sofa with a determined smile. "I almost wish the royal divorce trial was still going on," she said.

The new king, George IV's, efforts to divorce his long-estranged wife, Caroline of Brunswick, had been the talk of London for months. The trial before the House of Lords had gone on for months and had formed the basis of two of their group's murder investigations, which had touched on attempts to affect the outcome. Yet Mélanie could feel a palpable relief in the group in her library as the conversation turned to the royal divorce.

"And glad as I am that the queen prevailed, I do wish the bill had been defeated instead of the government's withdrawing it," Edith added.

"Once the Tory's majority was down to nine, they didn't have much choice," Malcolm said. The Tories, the ruling party, had backed the king in the divorce proceedings. The Whigs had supported the queen, partly in hopes of ousting the Tories from power, partly because popular opinion had coalesced round the queen. And at least in some cases because they genuinely believed she had been ill-used. "But I'm only an observer from the Commons. What do you think, Julien?"

Julien Mallinson, who had recently assumed the title of Earl Carfax after a quarter century undercover, grinned. "I may sit in the Lords but I make no pretense to understanding them. You're much more versed in the inner workings of the party."

Malcolm snorted. "I'm not even a proper Whig, to hear most of them talk."

"You're a more proper Whig than most of us." Raoul O'Roarke, who was Malcolm's father (and also Mélanie's former spymaster, though that was another story), settled back on the settee and took a drink of coffee. "But as someone used to the field, I'd say the Tories knew when to concede to avoid embarrassment."

Raoul's wife, Laura, turned to him with a smile. "And you have known the prime minister longer than any of us."

Raoul, a Radical and revolutionary, who had formed an unlikely alliance with the prime minister, Lord Liverpool, when they were both in their twenties, gave an ironic smile. "I can't claim to be privy to the inner workings of his mind. But I will say he's always struck me as a pragmatist. He hadn't just lost votes like Granville and Trenchard, he'd lost arch-Tories like Stafford. Harrowby didn't vote at all and he's in the cabinet. Withdrawing the case may have angered the king, but probably not as much as losing would have done."

"But it has yet to bring the government down," Edith said. Her eyes were bright, partly with genuine interest, partly, Mélanie suspected, with a desperate need for distraction.

"I'd love to see that," Laura said, "but having grown up with uprisings in India, I rather suspect popular attention will move on. And the Tories will remain in power." She smiled at Edith, with whom she currently ran the school they had all started on a property Mélanie and Malcolm owned.

"You always have the best insights, Laura," Edith said. "For once, I found myself wanting to believe in fairy tales. At least that sort of fairy tale." She took a resolute sip of coffee. "I long since ceased believing in the other sort."

Julien pushed himself to his feet and moved to the drinks trolley. "I think you could do with something stronger." He picked up a whisky decanter and splashed some into her coffee.

Edith grinned at him. "You know just what to say, Lord Carfax."

"And you should know better than to call me 'Lord Carfax.' If anything—"

A ring sounded from the hall. Malcolm jumped up and went into the hall to the front door. Mélanie followed her husband, wondering if it was the source of a new investigation or a social caller who would be shocked by their habit of answering their own door in the evenings. Over Malcolm's shoulder she saw a tall figure in a sodden greatcoat and beaver hat. "I'm sorry." Thomas Thornsby, the man who had recently betrothed himself to Marianne Schofield rather than Edith, pulled his hat from his head. It was dripping rainwater. "I have no right to be here."

"Of course you have a right to be here," Malcolm said. "You're a friend. You'd better come in."

"I'm afraid I'm a mess."

"Nonsense," Mélanie said. "Though why don't you give us your greatcoat and hat."

He gave a bleak smile. "You're kind, Mrs. Rannoch. I fear I don't deserve it."

"Don't be silly, Thomas," Edith said from the library doorway. "We're all still friends."

Thomas started, then turned and met her gaze for a moment without flinching.

"I'm sorry," Edith said. "You probably didn't know I was here."

"No, that is—I wouldn't have troubled you if I'd known. Wouldn't have wanted to. But I wouldn't have had a choice."

Edith drew a breath. "What is it?"

Thomas's hands clenched on his sodden greatcoat as he slid it from his shoulders. "It's Miss Schofield—Marianne."

"Something's wrong?" Edith asked. "I mean—"

"Yes. No." Thomas stared down at the greatcoat in his hands, dripping rainwater onto the black-and-white marble tiles. "I can't be sure. But she's disappeared."

élanie drew in her breath and heard Malcolm do the same. "Perhaps we'd better go into the library," she said. "I suspect we're going to need everyone's help."

She set Thomas's greatcoat and hat on the bench where they all dumped their damp outerwear, and they moved into the library. The rest of the company were politely silent but had obviously heard most, if not all. Julien gave Thomas a cup of whisky-laced coffee. Thomas sat on a solitary straight-backed chair. Edith returned to her seat beside Cordelia on one of the settees. Well away from Thomas. The children, who were playing at the far end of the room, with Malcolm's secretary Sandy and his wife Bet and Berowne the cat, looked up with curiosity. Colin, Mélanie and Malcolm's seven-year-old son, met Mélanie's gaze for a moment, then inclined his head and returned to their game, drawing the others with him.

Malcolm moved back to the Queen Anne chair where he and Mélanie had been sitting. "Disappeared?" he asked.

Thomas took a deep drink of coffee and whisky. Almost a gulp. Which was very unlike him. "We were at Lady Cowper's." He looked round the group. "I rather thought—"

"Yes," Mélanie said, perching on the arm of the chair where Malcolm was sitting. "We were all invited. But it's a busy time with the holidays fast approaching. I think we all preferred a quiet evening."

Thomas gave a quick nod. "I confess I'd have preferred a quiet evening myself. I think perhaps Marianne might have done as well. She's careful of her feelings, but she seems to enjoy quiet. It had been—it was a hectic evening. We weren't together all the time, of course. But I know Miss Scho—Marianne—went out into the garden for some air. Before the rain started. And no one's seen her since."

"Are you sure?" Cordelia asked. "I mean, it's easy to get lost at a ball—"

Thomas took another quick drink of coffee and whisky. "Her friend Miss Wilcox went outside with her. They've been best friends since they were children. But then Miss Wilcox came back in because she was promised for a dance. I saw her when she came back in. She told me Marianne had said she'd just be a few minutes longer. But no one saw her come back in. No one has seen her since."

"You're sure she's not somewhere in the Cowpers' house?" Mélanie asked. She had been there many times for balls and she could well remember the crowds and chaos during a ball, on the stairs, in the antechambers and sitting rooms. A successful ball was inevitably a great crush, and Emily's balls were always successful. "She could have been overwhelmed by the heat or taken ill in some way—"

"We've looked everywhere." Thomas clunked his silver-rimmed cup into its saucer.

"Who's 'we'?" Harry asked.

"Miss Wilcox, who found me. She noticed Marianne was missing just about the same time I became concerned and started looking for her. We didn't want to create a scandal or to disturb her parents."

"It's possible she went to the retiring room and then was overcome by the heat or other things," Cordelia said.

"Yes, we did think of that. Miss Wilcox checked right away, and we looked in all the antechambers in which she might have taken refuge. We're both convinced she's not in the house." He looked round the company. "I know I'm not an investigator or an agent, but I have assisted you. I don't think Marianne is in the house."

"Marriage can be a momentous decision," Cordelia said. "If Miss Schofield was nervous and needed time to think—"

"Yes, I've thought of that." Thomas gripped the handle of his cup and turned it in its saucer. "In truth, Miss Schofield and I haven't had much time to talk. She assured me she was happy with our betrothal—"

"Did you tell her you were?" Julien asked.

Thomas's gaze shot to Julien's face. "Of course. What's that to say to anything?"

Julien added more whisky to Thomas's coffee. "Merely that you obviously weren't."

Thomas's cup tilted in his fingers. He righted it, as droplets of coffee and whisky spattered into the saucer. "I don't believe I made any false statements to Marianne. Neither of us had—have—illusions that we're making a love match. But I thought we could deal together well. I would never—She assured me she had no desire for anything more romantic than what is between us."

"And you believed her?" Kitty said. She was leaning close to Julien as she said it, her intimacy with her husband palpable.

"I—had no reason not to do so." Thomas stared at his hands. "I begin to question everything."

"Does Miss Schofield have enemies?" Malcolm asked.

Thomas's head jerked up. "Enemies? Marianne?"

"It's something to consider when someone disappears," Malcolm said.

"Good God, surely you aren't suggesting Marianne was kidnapped? From Lady Cowper's garden at a ball?"

"It doesn't seem likely," Malcolm said. "But it's a possibility to consider."

Thomas glanced round the room. "I know you're all agents. I've seen enough to know you live in a world I can't even begin to understand. But that isn't Marianne's world. Not remotely."

"People don't always stay neatly in their worlds," Cordelia said. "As we have cause to know. It wasn't my world either, once."

"Yes, I do understand that," Thomas said, "but—"

"I've lived a more adventurous life than Marianne? I do concede that."

Thomas flushed, not surprising given the nature of Cordelia's adventures. "That's not what I meant. But Marianne has led quite a sheltered life. I can't imagine her being involved in those sorts of intrigues. And I certainly don't know of any enemies she had."

"She's an heiress," Julien said. "She must have been much sought-after before her betrothal to you."

Thomas took a measured sip of coffee and whisky. "She had suitors. I can't say I know any of them well."

"Did any of them take losing her particularly ill?"

Thomas clunked down his cup. "You think she was abducted to force a marriage?"

"It wouldn't be the first time it's happened," Julien said.

Thomas passed a hand over his face. "That seems more likely than that she's involved in espionage. I'm trying to think of the other gentlemen I've seen her dance with, the others who called at her parents' house when I was there. I can't imagine any of them doing such a thing. I realize that may be a failure of my imagination. But Marianne's a level-headed young woman. For someone to force her into a carriage or the like from the garden at a ball—"

"Do you think she might have run off on her own account?" Kitty asked.

Thomas met her gaze without flinching. Either from the question or, perhaps more importantly, from his own fears. "Because she didn't want to marry me, you mean?"

"The engagement would be the likeliest reason for her to have run off, though not the only one." Kitty's look managed to be kind without evading the question. "Is it possible she's in love with someone else?"

Thomas drew in and released his breath. Across the room Edith had gone completely still. "Marianne and I were both—free of romantic illusions when it came to our betrothal. She gave every indication that she was comfortable with that. That was what she wanted. But I can't claim—I can't say that she confided in me. I can't really say I knew—know—her innermost thoughts. So it's possible. I can't be sure she wasn't—isn't—in love with someone else. She might have accepted me because she knew her parents wanted it. She might have felt the only way she could be with the person she loved was to elope. I'd have hoped she'd have told me if that were the case. But I doubt she would have done."

"I doubt most people would tell their betrothed if they were going to elope with someone else," Cordelia said. "If they were on such terms with that person, they'd never have become betrothed in the first place."

"Did she seem afraid of anything?" Raoul asked. "Or afraid in general?"

Thomas frowned. "The Schofields live—not a quiet life, but I suppose you'd say a conventional life. Her mother's been concerned about the protests over the queen's trial, but Marianne didn't seem to pay much heed to them. She tended to be the one to soothe her mother when she got agitated about them." He pressed his hands over his eyes. "The truth is, I can't really claim to know Marianne at all."

Mélanie reached for the cup of coffee she'd left on the sofa table. "Did anything unusual happen during the evening? Before Miss Schofield disappeared?"

Thomas turned his coffee cup on its saucer. "There was one thing. I don't know that you'd call it unusual, but it was uncomfortable. Lady Cowper had decorated for the holiday season. Holly branches in vases and red and green draperies and that sort of thing. There was a bunch of mistletoe in the doorway from the ballroom to the supper room. Marianne and I walked beneath it when we left the dance floor and one of Marianne's brother's friends said the newly betrothed couple should kiss. We just shook our heads and would have moved on but there was such a crowd we couldn't move quickly. And then other people took up the chant—there was a group of undergraduates about us. Not Gerry, Marianne's brother. He's quite sensible. But the sort who are—"

"Annoying," Harry said.

Thomas nodded. "I was uncomfortable, but, more than that, I could tell Marianne was uncomfortable. I wouldn't for the world put her in an uncomfortable situation. But we couldn't move away and more and more people were joining the crowd and taking up the chant, and it was starting to feel as though the whole ballroom was staring at us. So finally I kissed her cheek. Marianne flushed and then looked me as though she was—I can't quite say. Perhaps embarrassed. Perhaps grateful. Perhaps both. Then she pressed my hand and slipped off through the crowd because she was promised for another dance. Or so she said."

"I take it you've never kissed her?" Julien asked.

Thomas shot a look at him.

"Sorry," Julien said, "it's none of my business, or it wouldn't be in the general run of things, but now we're in the midst of an investigation, so everything's rather changed."

"No," Thomas said. "I never—we never had. It isn't—it didn't seem to be part of our betrothal."

Across the room, Edith was staring into her coffee cup as though the dregs were a subject of the greatest fascination. Had she and Thomas ever kissed? Mélanie couldn't be sure, but she rather suspected they had. Thomas wouldn't have initiated it, but Edith very likely would have done.

"Awkward to have to face the pressure of a first kiss in public," Kitty said. "Perhaps that was all there was to her reaction."

"Perhaps." Thomas glanced at his hands. "But for a moment I wondered if she was as content with our betrothal as she appeared. For a moment I wondered—" He broke off.

"What?" Cordelia asked.

"If I knew her at all."

"Did you have other reasons to think you didn't know her?" Laura asked.

"I—" Thomas drew in and released his breath. "Marianne's brother introduced us. He's studying classics at Cambridge and he comes to some Classicists' Society talks. Marianne's charming and we enjoyed talking. But I can't say—I can't claim to know her well. I thought we both wanted the same things when it came to marriage. But for a moment tonight I wondered if that was my own assumption. If what I saw as restraint was really genuine doubt. If she didn't so much want the life her parents wanted for her as think she had no other choice than to accept it." His knuckles whitened. "We have much to discuss. But for right now I need to find Marianne and make sure she is safe and well. That takes precedence over everything."

Mélanie pushed herself to her feet. "We were invited to the Cowpers' tonight. We didn't accept, but I doubt we'll be turned away."

Thomas looked up, a mixture of fear and hope in his gaze.

"That's why you came, isn't it?" Mélanie asked. "Because you want our help?"

"I desperately need your help. In truth, I'm not sure what else to do next. But I didn't want to ask—"

"I can't speak for the others," Mélanie said, "but give me five minutes to make myself presentable for the ballroom and I'm with you."

She looked round the room, but the others were already on their feet as well. Including Edith. Edith spoke for all of them. "Of course. What are friends for?"

CHAPTER 3

*M*usic and candlelight spilled from the Cowpers' house into George Street. Carriages lined the street, the horses' breath frosting in the December air as the coachmen waited to take their employers home. Mélanie, Malcolm, and the others had elected to walk from Berkeley Square. Much faster than navigating the crush of carriages. They climbed the front steps between flambeaux. Two footmen were on duty at the door. One, who appeared to have been hired for evening, seemed confused at their lack of presence on the guest list, but the other, one of the Cowpers' regular staff who knew them all well, ushered them in without a blink and took their outer things.

"Her ladyship isn't greeting guests on the stairs any longer," he said, "but I'm sure she'll be most pleased to see you. I think you'll find her in the ballroom."

Ladies in gowns of velvet or shimmering satin or gauzy silk or muslin and gentlemen in dark coats and scarlet uniform jackets crowded the stairs and spilled into the hall from the card and smoking rooms downstairs. The strains of a waltz drifted down the stairs twining with the chatter of voices, the clink of crystal, the patter of satin slippers and Cordoba leather soles on marble. Puffs of smoke came from the smoking room. The smell of pine boughs and French scent and close-pressed bodies filled the air. The sights and sounds and smells of a Mayfair ball. A milieu Mélanie had lived in for the first six years of her marriage. She spent less time in it these days but it still brought the intoxication of a glass of champagne and at the same time a sense of walls closing in.

"It's going to take half an hour just to get up the stairs," Cordelia murmured as the footman took her velvet cloak. "Emily's ball is obviously a great success."

"So the obvious solution is to reconnoiter." Raoul turned to the footman. "Could you direct us to the back stairs? I assure you we wouldn't ask were the situation not desperate."

Five minutes later, after a bit of time navigating the hall, they went up a flight of simple pine stairs and through a baize-covered door to the upstairs passage where the buzz of voices and crystal and music were even louder. Thomas and Edith, the least used to investigating, followed without a blink. "We should talk to Miss Wilcox first," Mélanie said as they emerged into the passage.

"I'll find her," Thomas said. "She's been hoping I'd bring you."

"We won't stray far," Malcolm said. "But we'll see what we can learn while you find her."

Investigating at a ball was second nature to all of them. Even Raoul, whom Mélanie had met in the midst of the Peninsular War but who was far more at home in Mayfair than she had ever realized.

Julien glanced towards the ballroom. "Someone should take a look outside while the rest of you stay close enough to talk to Miss Wilcox. Care for some reconnaissance, Kitkat?"

"Excellent idea," his wife said.

"If she went outside from the ballroom, she probably went down from the balcony," Raoul said. "Why don't you look at the balcony. Laura and I'll go back down the stairs and start in the garden."

~

"MÉLANIE! " Emily Cowper swept up in a stir of emerald green velvet and caught Mélanie's arm as Mélanie navigated the passage outside the ballroom. "You told me you couldn't come."

"Yes, and it was shocking of us to come without responding properly." Mélanie leaned forwards to kiss Emily's cheek. "Do forgive us."

"Stuff. As though you aren't welcome any night of the week." Emily drew back and ran her gaze over Mélanie. "I do like your hair. It's different tonight."

Mélanie had stuck a diamond diadem on her loose hair to hold it in place and give a semblance of an evening coiffure. "I didn't have Blanca's help tonight." Blanca and her husband Miles Addison, Malcolm's valet, and their son were away visiting Addison's family for the holidays.

"You'll set a new fashion. People will start spending hours making their hair tumble with artful abandon. I like the gown too. Have I seen it before?"

"Not exactly like this." She'd wrapped a silver-figured claret velvet overdress over the wine-colored silk slip she'd been wearing for their dinner party.

Emily's gaze shifted over Mélanie's face. "Something's happened, hasn't it? You wouldn't be here otherwise. I don't know whether to feel pleased or alarmed that my ball is the center of intrigue. Is someone passing secret information in one of my anterooms?"

"Nothing like that." Mélanie hesitated. Thomas hadn't asked them to keep Marianne Schofield's disappearance secret, but it had certainly been implied. And yet, who to know the inner workings of a ballroom better than the hostess. "Thomas

Thornsby is concerned because Marianne Schofield seems to be missing."

Emily's eyes opened wide. "She ran off?"

"Thomas isn't sure. Apparently he and her friend Miss Wilcox looked all over the house for her."

"You know how easy it is to get lost at a ball. I made it a point not to have my mother see me all night if I could manage it."

"Yes. But Thomas is most concerned. And he's not fanciful."

Emily's brows tightened. "Thomas Thornsby isn't the sort of man who would have appealed to me when I was in my first season. Or even in the early years of my marriage. I'd have written him off as dull. But now I must say I can see the attraction. There's something about that quiet intelligence. A bit like Malcolm. Though without the danger. Don't look at me like that, Mélanie, you can't deny there's an edge of danger about Malcolm. He lives in it. So do you. The danger is undeniably appealing, but so is the quiet intelligence. In any case, I can quite see now why Edith Simmons used to follow Mr. Thornsby round the room with her gaze. I wasn't particularly happy to learn about his betrothal to Marianne Schofield."

"Nor was I," Mélanie said.

Emily fingered the sticks of her fan. "Odd, on the surface they seem well-suited. Both quiet, neither the sort to cause a stir or cut a dash, and I think Miss Schofield has a good understanding. But there's something missing between them. Something I don't think I even quite realized existed when I married Cowper." She slid the fan through her fingers. "Odd how one's feelings on that sort of thing can change. Not that I regret what I have, mind you. How could I, with my children and so much agreeable about my life? But I'm not sure it's precisely the path I want for my children in matrimony."

"They'll have more ability to choose," Mélanie said.

"I hope so. I must say, I quite wish it were Mr. Thornsby who'd run off and not Miss Schofield."

"We don't know that she has run off," Mélanie said. "But yes, so do I."

"It's want of fortune, I suppose. That prevents his running off with Miss Simmons or simply marrying her in the conventional way." Emily's expertly tended brows knotted. "One knows how beastly lack of fortune can be for marital options, but one doesn't quite feel it until one sees one's friends going through it, if you know what I mean."

"Yes. Did you see Miss Schofield tonight?"

"I greeted the whole family on the stairs. They were among the first arrivals. They have the punctuality of those new to the beau monde," said Emily, with the careless ease of one born to it.

"Did you notice anything amiss?"

"No. That is, I confess my mind was on the arrangements in the supper room and if the holly and flowers were quite the right shade with the wall-hangings—candlelight does change the look of things so—and if I'd gone too far with the holiday theme, so I wasn't paying as much attention as I might have done. The younger sister looked a bit overwhelmed—she just came out in September and she's not a diamond of the first water like Marianne, I fear. Marianne was quiet as usual. She has beautiful manners but one can never quite tell what's going on in her head. I remember thinking that I doubted she was madly in love with Thomas Thornsby, but that if she were, I wasn't sure one would be able to tell. It should serve her well in society. But it's not very helpful for gauging the inner workings of her mind."

"And later in the evening?"

Emily frowned down at her green silk fan. "She and Thomas danced. Two dances and they appeared in good spirits, but then they both danced with other people—quite as if they weren't betrothed at all. I quite applaud that they aren't the sort of couple that sit in each other's pockets all night—you know the engaged couples who scarcely seem to know anyone else is in the room and really one wonders why they take the trouble to go to a ball at all—but it did all seem a bit tepid. Then I saw her talking with her friend Miss Wilcox later in the evening." Emily paused in consideration. "That was about eleven, I should think. I didn't see her after. But really, there are scores of people here I haven't seen at all. That's a true sign of a ball being a success. It's too crowded and chaotic for the hostess to have the least idea of what's happening or even who is present." Her gaze flickered over Mélanie's face. "What on earth do you think happened to her?"

"I don't know. You didn't happen to notice the way she was looking at any of the other gentlemen she danced with, did you?"

"You think she eloped?"

"It's an obvious explanation, but sometimes the obvious explanation is the correct one."

"Good heavens, I thought the king and queen had already eclipsed any other possible scandal this season, but an elopement in the midst of a ball might do it. I can't say I noticed anything in particular. But I was hardly looking for those sorts of clues. If anyone could hide her feelings well, it's Marianne Schofield. And if she was planning to elope, she'd certainly attempt to hide her feelings. Where was she last seen?"

"In the garden. She told Miss Wilcox she'd be in shortly."

"They were in the garden? In December?"

"She was a bit overset it seems. There'd been a fuss about her and Mr. Thornsby and the mistletoe."

"Oh dear. I heard some shouts but I didn't know whom it concerned. Poor girl. No one should have to kiss anyone in public. I'll talk to the footmen. Discreetly."

"Thank you."

"Does her family know?"

"No, only Mr. Thornsby and Miss Wilcox. And they're trying to keep it that way."

"I quite understand. Family can hopelessly get in the way. I certainly wouldn't have wanted mine anywhere near if I were trying to elope. Though I suppose Miss Schofield wouldn't want us near either. Are we trying to stop her from eloping?"

"We're trying to discover why she disappeared," Mélanie said. "If she's safe and left of her own free will, I certainly wouldn't attempt to convince her to come back."

"Nor would I," Emily said.

"You don't sound like a patroness of Almack's." Where Laura couldn't have vouchers because she was divorced and the Duke of Wellington had been turned away for wearing trousers instead of knee breeches.

"Stuff." Emily tapped Mélanie on the arm with her fan. "You should know better than anyone that there's the public face one turns to the world. And then there's who one really is."

Which was remarkably apt. Especially as Emily didn't have the least idea Mélanie had been a French spy.

CHAPTER 4

"*D*amnable watching Thornsby and Edith try to be practical and pragmatic," Julien murmured to Kitty as they made their way along the edge of the ballroom to the French windows onto the balcony. "Particularly Edith, who had no say in the matter."

"I actually think Edith seems rather better now there's something to do," Kitty said. "Even if it does involve Miss Schofield. At the beginning of the evening, she was trying to avoid our pitying looks."

"I've never looked pitying in my life." Julien took Kitty's hand as they slid past a trio of dowagers.

"You feel for her. Don't deny it, darling."

"Of course I feel for her." Julien turned the handle of the French window. "I also feel for Miss Schofield. It's not easy being married for one's fortune. I saw what it did to my mother. Not that I blame Thornsby. He's doing what he thinks he needs to do for his family."

"I feel for her as well," Kitty said. "And for Thomas. And Edith. I could wish Thomas would make a different decision, but I can see it's damnably hard to do so."

"The whole thing is a damnable coil." Julien stood aside to allow her to precede him onto the balcony. "What a fortunate thing it is that I had a fortune to offer you along with my hand."

"You didn't have the fortune when you proposed," Kitty reminded him, stepping into a shock of cool air. "You didn't even have a legal name, and we were possibly going to have to flee the country and live incognito."

"And you secretly hoped we would have to do just that."

"Possibly. No, not really." Kitty clicked the window shut. "I was getting to like London and our friends and I wanted to see what you could do in Parliament."

"Ha."

"You've done a remarkable amount already. The point is, I didn't marry you for your prospects. You didn't have any prospects. I didn't even know the life we'd be living. On the other hand, I knew we had the resources to manage not to starve. And I didn't have younger siblings I felt the need to provide for. Or parents and a crumbling ancestral estate to worry about. So I do understand Mr. Thornsby's position."

They moved to the edge of the balcony and looked down at the garden. Hung with colored lanterns, but empty of guests. Kitty drew her shawl about her as a gust of wind cut the air. She'd worn a rather daring new dress to the Rannochs' for dinner. Gold silk, cut on clinging lines, with thin straps for sleeves and narrow ruffles running down the front and round the low-cut bodice. Not precisely a ballgown, though the drama helped it pass as one, and definitely not suited to the outdoors in December. Not that most dresses she'd seen in the ballroom were. The balcony railing was still wet from the earlier rain. "It's a cool night to spend time outside. She must have had strong reasons to escape the ballroom."

"She'd been forced to kiss Thornsby."

"Sharing a first kiss—perhaps a first kiss with anyone—in

public would be beastly. Even if one wanted to kiss the person in question."

"Yes, but I have the distinct sense Miss Schofield didn't want to kiss Thornsby."

"Yes, so do I. Given that he's not in love with her, I suppose it's a good thing she isn't in love with him." Kitty looked over the balcony rail and caught the flash of Laura's crimson velvet gown and then Raoul blending into the shadows. "Anything?"

"Not yet," Raoul said. "We could use your help."

They went down the side stairs to the garden, which Kitty remembered being full of delightful walks and brilliant flowers at spring, summer, and autumn entertainments. Now the trees made a dark tracery against the gray-black sky and the bushes were leafless shadows. Rainwater glistened on the paving stones in the lamplight.

"There are traces of thread on that bench." Raoul held up a lantern and gestured towards a stone bench. "That's where Miss Schofield and Miss Wilcox sat to talk, presumably."

"I'm the first to want to escape a ball," Laura said. "And I know I grew up in India. But it's distinctly cold for a tête-à-tête."

"It's crowded in the ballroom," Kitty said. "Probably even in the antechambers and salons. We thought she might have wanted to escape after the mistletoe incident. And to talk to her friend. The garden's one place they could have counted on privacy."

"And she stayed outside because she didn't want to face the crowd yet?" Laura said. "That's plausible."

"Or she stayed outside because she had a plan to leave," Julien said.

Kitty glanced round the walls of the garden. Used to seeking out exits in shadows, she could just make out a gate in the wall opposite that must lead to the mews. "That would require a lot of planning. Well before the incident with the mistletoe."

"Unless the incident with the mistletoe was set up to create a diversion," Laura said. "Thomas said one of Miss Schofield's brother's friends started calling for them to kiss. I was thinking how beastly that young man was, but he could have been a friend of Miss Schofield's as well."

Julien shot a smile at Laura. "I love how devious your mind is."

Laura returned the smile. "I know what it's like to be a young woman in want of escape. Assuming that's why she disappeared."

"It wouldn't be a bad time to stage an escape," Kitty said. "No one ever knows quite where anyone is at a ball. Her disappearance might not have been discovered until the early hours of the morning when her family prepared to go home."

"It would have taken a lot of planning," Laura said. "And her best friend seemingly doesn't know the truth. She's involved in the search."

"Unless it was Thornsby who figured out she was missing and enlisted Miss Wilcox," Julien said. "Then she wouldn't have had much choice but to play along."

Raoul was crouched down with the lantern, examining the ground. He pushed aside some blades of grass, slid his fingers between the paving stones, and held something up. Gold and pale pink glittered in the lantern light. An earring.

Kitty examined it. The back had sprung open. "I've lost plenty of earrings in gardens. Not just that way," she added, as her husband flashed a grin. "It could have got caught on her shawl or a branch and slipped off. Or it could have come off in a struggle if someone grabbed her. Assuming it's her earring."

Raoul was frowning down at the earring. "Sweetheart?" Laura said. "What is it?"

"Nothing, perhaps. Or perhaps a great deal. I didn't care to go into this in front of Thornsby, but I'm not a complete stranger to the Schofield family. I know Miss Schofield's father." His gaze moved to Julien. "Had you heard of him?"

"No," Julien said. "But then I was hardly in the inner circle of French intelligence the way you were."

"Depends on how one defines inner circle. You were very close to key players on both sides." Including Josephine Bonaparte, who had been Julien's lover before she married the future emperor.

"Being close to both sides can rather interfere with how much information one gets from both," Julien said. "Schofield was an agent?"

Raoul hesitated. Kitty understood. A spymaster's instincts were to protect his people. Even from friends. Even after the war was over. But Raoul was the first to admit the chess board had shifted. "Let's say he passed information."

"He made munitions," Laura said. "Did he—"

"Provide the British with faulty munitions?" Raoul said. "No. But because he had contracts from the army, he had information about British troop movements. He gave those to the French. Or, I should say, sold them."

"And when he made a fortune betting the right way on the news from Waterloo—" Kitty said.

"It wasn't a gamble," Raoul said in a level voice. "He had colleagues on the French side who sent him word. He knew the French had been routed. One could say he had a right to profit on the knowledge. Save that he was profiting at the expense of others who didn't have the same knowledge. I don't think much more of the new world based on commerce than I did of the old world based on birth. But if one is going to play the game, the chess board should at least be even."

"My god, O'Roarke," Julien said. "The chess board is never even. If you've learned nothing else, haven't you learned that? Whether it's birth or fortune that matters, someone finds a way to tip it in their direction. We live in a world that's rotten to the core. Whether we're talking about bankers or aristocrats."

Kitty watched her husband in the shadows. The savagery was always just under the surface with him. But it wasn't often he let it loose. "And yet you choose to live in that world," she said.

He shot a look at her. "I have a wife who convinced me change is possible. And children have a way of preventing one from walking away completely." He perched on the stone wall between the terrace and the lawn and folded his arms across his chest. "Sorry, didn't mean to wallow."

"You have a right to," Raoul said. "But as to how all this could relate to Miss Schofield's running off—"

"You think someone threatened her over her father's actions?" Laura asked.

"Possibly," Raoul said. "But to what end? If someone wanted money, presumably they'd have gone straight to her father."

"What if the blackmailer wanted to break up the betrothal," Laura said. "We keep thinking about Edith and Thomas, and though I confess to a distinct bias where Edith is concerned, it strains my imagination to think of her using blackmail to break up the betrothal."

"Mine too," Kitty said. "But Miss Schofield had a number of suitors, as we've heard it. Someone else could have tried to break them apart. For that matter, someone else could have wanted Thomas to marry elsewhere."

"Such as Lady Shroppington?" Julien suggested.

The name landed in the cold garden air with the thud of a rock tossed onto the slate paving stones. Lady Shroppington, Thomas's great-aunt, had presumably cut her ties with the immediate family when they learned she'd been behind the murder of Thomas's brother, Lewis. And yet her desire to manipulate her family had never been plainer.

"Surely she wouldn't think of Thomas as her heir now," Laura said. "Thomas wouldn't accept her fortune if she offered it to him."

"She may not realize that," Raoul said. "And with Alistair gone, she's bound to turn her energies in a new direction. Even if she doesn't consider Thomas an heir, she might take an interest in his marriage."

"Something that forced Miss Schofield away in the midst of a ball is audacious enough to be Lady Shroppington's work," Kitty said.

Julien cast a glance up at the ballroom. The candlelight suddenly had the glitter of shards of glass. "So it could."

31

Malcolm had disappeared. So had Harry and Cordy and Edith. They were all bent on uncovering new information, as they should be. Mélanie glanced round the passage, nodded at Harriet Granville and Hetty and James Trenchard, exchanged a few words with Lady Castlereagh, who had been very kind to her at the Congress of Vienna though her husband and Malcolm had been at political loggerheads, and moved down the passage looking for someone it would be helpful to talk to. The scope of this investigation was smaller than their usual sort of case, which typically touched on politics and international diplomacy—and, inevitably, espionage.

"Mrs. Rannoch."

The voice stopped Mélanie before she turned her head and met the piercing blue gaze set beneath plucked brows and white plumes held in place with a diamond clip. Lady Shroppington was not a tall woman, but she could command a room. Her white satin gown, which might have looked absurdly girlish, instead gave her the look of an avenging goddess. She had stopped beside a Chinese vase filled with holly branches, which she somehow managed to make into an imposing backdrop.

"I suppose this was inevitable," she said.

"Lady Shroppington." Mélanie took a step forwards. Even though it felt like moving towards a menace. "I confess I've been expecting to see you again." The last time they met, Lady Shroppington had exited Berkeley Square after her first, and likely only, visit, accompanied by her son Alistair Rannoch, who had made every effort to turn Malcolm and Mélanie out and reclaim the house. Of course, technically it was his house, as Malcolm had only inherited the house when Alistair, his putative father, was presumed dead. Thwarted in his attempts to rehabilitate his name, Alistair had then fled the country. Presumably. None of them knew precisely where he was.

"I spent some time in the country," Lady Shroppington said, as though none of those events had occurred. "At a certain point, the trial consuming London became tedious. One could scarcely go out of doors without encountering protesters or scurrilous cartoons or comments in bad taste from one's friends. And I'm not sure which was worse." Her gaze skimmed over Mélanie. "I didn't think you frequented balls much these days."

"Emily Cowper is a dear friend." Which was perfectly true.

Lady Shroppington's mouth thinned. "For a patroness of Almack's, Emily's standards are very broad."

"She has a wonderful tolerance for human foibles."

"A charming if regrettably broad-minded way of putting it."

Mélanie moved to the side, partly to hear better, partly to avoid the crowd milling in the passage and moving in and out of the ballroom just beyond. "What brought you back to London?"

"At some point one has to face society. Or one feels quite cut off. And I learned my great-nephew was betrothed. Naturally, that made me wish to see the family."

That was brazen, considering that Lady Shroppington had been behind the murder of Thomas's younger brother and she knew Mélanie knew she had been behind it. It also put Lady

Shroppington squarely in the midst of the current investigation. "Are you pleased about the betrothal?" Mélanie asked.

"That's hardly your affair, Mrs. Rannoch. I will say that it's high time Thomas chose a wife. Family matter."

"That's something we agree about. However one defines family. Acknowledged or unacknowledged."

Lady Shroppington was several inches shorter than Mélanie, but she suddenly seemed to be looking down her nose. "I'm sure I don't know what you're talking about."

"My dear Lady Shroppington. Since you've plainly taken the trouble to seek me out, I assume we aren't going to pretend the events of last October didn't occur."

Lady Shroppington's sharp brows drew together. "Surely whatever your origins, you've lived in the beau monde long enough to know we've elevated ignoring uncomfortable events to an art."

"But I thought you prided yourself on being plainspoken about love affairs."

Lady Shroppington's brows tightened.

"Of course," Mélanie said. "It wasn't about love at all. At least, not at first."

Lady Shroppington gave a short laugh. "You would think that, my dear. Surely we can dispense with the pretense that I don't know the truth about you and your sorry excuse of a marriage. Though I should perhaps make you my compliments on having managed to make it last. There are worse bargains struck at every ball in Mayfair."

Mélanie's hands stilled on the folds of her gown. The silver embroidery cut her fingers. There was a time when the realization that someone knew the truth of her past would have sent a chill of panic through her. Before Malcolm learned the truth, it threatened the end of her marriage. After he knew, it threatened the wreck of their life in Britain and her husband's career. Which, she had feared, would destroy their marriage. But now she had a royal pardon, and if the truth coming out would still make their lives uncomfortable, it was not the threat it had once been. "My marriage is a lot of things, but it's no bargain."

"You're too clever for this, Mrs. Rannoch. Don't pretend to me of all people that you love him."

"Can you claim you didn't love the late Lord Carfax?"

"Love." Lady Shroppington's mouth curled round the words. "Do you think I even believe in it?"

"One doesn't necessarily have to believe in it to feel it."

Lady Shroppington's long fingers stilled on her ostrich feather fan. "It was never about him. I learned early on one can never lose sight of a goal."

"Knowing that doesn't mean one doesn't lose sight of it. Or that the goal doesn't change."

Lady Shroppington regarded Mélanie with a steady gaze that was not entirely adversarial. "You can't tell me you don't care about winning."

"Define winning. And winning at what?"

"You're a game player, Mrs. Rannoch. You can't tell me you'll ever leave the game."

God, was that even possible? There were times she'd have said she'd give anything to leave the espionage game. But in truth she couldn't say she wanted to. "Is that why you invented the Elsinore League? To stay in the game?"

A faint smile curved Lady Shroppington's mouth. "Tell me you can't imagine wanting power. Tell me you haven't wondered how a woman can achieve it. If I were you, I'd be driven mad that my husband didn't put his gifts to better use to secure more of it."

"That would rather depend on my goals. And his."

Lady Shroppington snorted. "Malcolm Rannoch at least has talents Shroppington didn't possess. I did what I could with him, but it mostly depended on his family name. I couldn't even persuade him to make anything of his seat in the Lords."

"I can imagine you wanted for occupation."

"Someone had the audacity to tell me it would have been different if I'd had children. But I can't imagine that. No one could expect children to fulfill a woman's interests."

Mélanie saw Colin and Jessica when she'd said goodnight after telling them she and Malcolm were unexpectedly going out. They hadn't been best pleased to be left at home, even with their friends and Sandy and Bet, whom they adored. "No," she agreed.

Lady Shroppington raised a brow. "I thought you'd put on a show as a devoted mother."

"I like to think I am devoted. But I think it would be asking too much of my children to expect them to provide all the interest in my life. And I don't think I could offer them nearly as much if I didn't have other interests. There's so much I can share with them." She regarded Lady Shroppington for a moment. "I imagine the League gave you something to share with Alistair."

Something shot through Lady Shroppington's gaze—regret, acknowledgement, affection? "The League were intended to make Alistair's fortune. It's not easy for a woman. It's not easy for a man without fortune or family either. But Alistair had a better chance of making something of himself than I did."

"Meaning you'd have liked to be prime minister yourself, but instead you could use your talents to get him the office."

"I never claimed—"

"No, I put that together. I imagine that was the plot after Trenchard achieved the office."

Lady Shroppington's mouth thinned. "You're very clever, Mrs. Rannoch. Don't make the mistake of thinking you're too clever."

"I'm looking at the results and working backwards. The Elsinore League members work together to empower each other. But you started the League for Alistair."

"Alistair started the League."

"Lady Shroppington. Don't deny your talents to me, of all people. Alistair is a very clever man. You're brilliant."

She saw a quick flash in Lady Shroppington's eyes, veiled shortly after. "You're too good for flattery."

"I see no need to flatter you. I don't particularly like you. I don't like you at all, if it comes to that. But I can't deny you are brilliant. I can admire brilliance. And I can appreciate how difficult it can be for a woman to find a scope for her talents."

Lady Shroppington's fingers tightened on her fan. "I imagine it was different for you. You were already used to selling yourself."

Mélanie was beyond being hurt by such comments. In theory. But she controlled a flinch. "One has more choice as a spy. I confess I found it quite a relief."

"It certainly brought you to a place I imagine you never thought to go."

"Yes. But I imagine that's true of most of us, for better or worse. I'm sure your work as an agent took you places you hadn't expected to go."

Lady Shroppington's brows lifted almost with amusement. "If you're trying to jolt me into confessions about the late Lord Carfax, I assure you you won't succeed. I see no point in discussing him."

"Do you discuss him with Alistair?"

"Why on earth would I talk to Alistair about his father? They had no connection except in biology."

"I'm not sure Alistair sees it that way."

"You can scarcely claim to know Alistair."

"No. But I've had a chance to observe his relationship with his half-brother."

"I'd hardly dignify the relationship with that term."

"Really? The rivalry is clear. On both sides. That's often a characteristic of brothers. And while I'd be the last to place importance on blood when it comes to family, Alistair's reaction to the Mallinson family implies he feels a connection. Which I imagine you do. Whatever you felt for the late Lord Carfax, you can't tell me you're indifferent."

"Even if I admitted to believing in anything as vulgar as romantic attachment, it's nothing one should build a life on."

"I'd have said that once."

"And now? You need the fairytale belief that your improbable marriage is a love match to justify the life you're living. I confess I'm disappointed in you."

"I can't imagine your being anything but disappointed in me."

Lady Shroppington's gaze narrowed, appraising but not necessarily disapproving. "We're antagonists, Mrs. Rannoch. But I have respect for what you've done. Admiration, even. I can understand why you went into your marriage and stayed in it. Pretending it's a grand love story seems beneath a woman of your understanding."

"Emotions aren't convenient. And can't be controlled."

"So says someone who's adopted the messy modern habit of letting them run roughshod over all sense." Lady Shroppington smoothed her skirts. "At least my great-nephew seems to have made a restrained choice."

"Have you met her?" Mélanie used every bit of her acting talents to keep her voice casual.

"I've met the family once or twice. They move in decent circles, whatever the origins of their fortune. I saw the girl tonight. A bit colorless, but she has looks and breeding. And from what I saw of her dancing with Thomas, they both have a sensible approach to matrimony. That should avoid disappointments."

"As you avoided them with Lord Shroppington?"

"Shroppington didn't have ambition. I should have seen that from the start. But then I had to choose among my possible suitors. A woman with a small dowry has limited options."

"So it's as much a game for a young lady in her first season as it is for a spy?"

Lady Shroppington drew a breath as though to make a quick rejoinder, then paused. "Of course it was a game. I'd have said

Carfax meant no more to me than any of the others. At least at the start. Even later, if I'd admitted to anything, it would have been the love of the game. Now— " She shrugged. "He might have been the love of my life. If I admitted to believing in anything remotely close to a love of one's life."

CHAPTER 6

Cordelia glanced round the passage outside the ballroom, then looked at her husband and Edith. "Time to make ourselves useful."

"You'll do better on your own," Harry said. "I'll see if I can find any classicists who know Gerry Schofield."

"I don't know that I'll know anyone useful," Edith said, "but I think I should circulate." She looked from Cordelia to Harry. "People may not want to mention Marianne Schofield in front of me. Polite reticence can be a damned nuisance."

Cordelia looked at Harry as Edith moved off. "I know it's foolish to interfere. I hope I'll be sensible enough not to interfere when it comes to Livia and Drusilla, and they at least are our daughters. We have even less right to interfere with Edith and Thomas. But I can't help—"

"Quite," Harry said. "Nothing like being happy oneself to want the same for others."

Cordelia felt herself smile. "That's one of the first times I've heard you say that."

"That I want others to be happy?"

"That you're happy."

"Oh. Well, perhaps I haven't said it in so many words. It's not the way I generally talk."

Cordelia looked up into her husband's blue eyes. So familiar and at times still so inscrutable. "To put it mildly."

"But you must know—Cordy, you can't doubt I'm happy. That I've been happier these past five years than ever before in my life."

"Yes. That is, no, of course I don't doubt it. But—"

"You wonder?"

Cordelia took a step closer to her husband. The crowd pressed close on all sides, lending an odd sort of privacy. "It's better now, isn't it? I mean—everything with George was beastly and despite everything he did, I'm sorry he's dead—but we got past something."

Harry reached for her hand. "I knew that investigation was going to change things. I wasn't at all sure it would change them for the better."

"But it did."

He squeezed her hand and lifted it to his lips. "I think so."

Cordelia smiled but kept her gaze on her husband's face. She felt as though she might crack in two if she breathed the wrong way. "It's never—"

"Everything in life is one day at a time, sweetheart."

"No happily-ever-afters?"

"Even those are one day at a time, I imagine. Until the princess and prince get hopelessly bored. One thing I'm quite sure of is that we'll never get bored."

"No, not that."

"But we came through something."

"Yes. And while I know nothing's settled, I don't think George can hurt us anymore. And not because he can't tell Livia the truth. Or his version of it."

Harry's fingers tightened round her own. "Nor do I. Now we can focus on our friends' romantic problem. And much as I feel for them, I confess that's a distinct relief."

"Malcolm." Hubert Mallinson stopped Malcolm as Mélanie was claimed by Emily Cowper. "What are you doing here?"

Malcolm regarded his former spymaster. "Attending a friend's ball."

"Why?"

"Does it need an explanation?"

"From you?" Hubert peered at Malcolm over his spectacles. "Yes. "

"I might ask you the same thing."

Hubert pushed the spectacles up on his nose. "Amelia and Lucinda wanted to attend. Or Amelia wanted to attend for Lucinda's sake. After complaining for years about not being allowed to attend balls, Lucinda seems to be finding them rather dull now that she's actually allowed to do so." Hubert tugged at the left earpiece of his spectacles. "What are you really doing here, Malcolm? Is it something to do with the aftermath of the queen's case?"

"No. I haven't heard anything new. Truly, though I don't suppose I'd tell you the truth if I had done. But this is nothing to do with the queen and king. That I know of."

"Is it to do with Alistair?" Hubert's gaze was hard, but Malcolm caught a flash behind the spectacle lenses. Even Hubert wasn't entirely immune to the fact that Alistair was his half-brother.

"No," Malcolm said.

"Lady Shroppington is here."

That was interesting. Last Malcolm had heard, she was in the country. "She was bound to come back sooner or later. We aren't here in search of her." Though any connection she might have to her great-nephew Thomas's betrothal was interesting. "It's minor. Trust me, Hubert. Hard as I know you find that to do."

Hubert grunted. "Probably easier than you find trusting me. If O'Roarke and Kitty are up to something to do with Spain—"

"No. That is, they may be, but if so, they haven't apprised me of it. We all felt like an evening out."

"When you lot feel like an evening out you embark on a mission."

"Not everything in life is a mission."

"That depends on whose life we're talking about. When it comes to a passel of spies—"

"I assure you our lives are much duller than you imagine."

"My dear Malcolm. You can convince me of a number of things. But not that your lives are dull."

"Have it your own way, sir."

"I should thank you," Hubert said. "The night looked to be crashingly dull and now I have you and Mélanie and your friends to keep an eye on. I'll appreciate the entertainment."

CHAPTER 7

"I found Miss Wilcox. She's in an antechamber down the passage." Thomas Thornsby stopped beside Mélanie, his gaze going after his great-aunt, who was just visible in the crowd.

"I just spoke with her," Mélanie said. "Lady Shroppington, that is. You hadn't seen her tonight?"

"No. I didn't realize she was back in London. Not that it signifies. We aren't on speaking terms."

"I'm not sure she sees it that way. She mentioned your betrothal and that she wanted to observe Miss Schofield."

"Did she?" Thomas's mild gaze hardened. "I can't imagine why. I'm not her heir. She's made it clear I won't be. And I've made it clear I wouldn't accept anything from her even if she chose to offer it. And that my sisters feel the same. I've tried to shield them, but they know about Lewis. At a certain point one has to warn even those one wants to protect against monsters."

"Very sensible," Mélanie said. "If more people in Gothic novels followed that advice, a great deal of drama would be avoided."

Thomas's gaze settled on her face. "Do you think—"

"I caught no hint that she'd had anything to do with Miss

Schofield's disappearance. But we can't ignore the possibility. I'll find Malcolm and the others."

She located her husband just outside the ballroom, frowning at the twists of red ribbon and green needles in a pine garland.

"Hubert," he said, meeting her gaze.

"Anything to do with this?" Mélanie asked.

"Not that I can tell. Just generally Hubert. You?"

"Lady Shroppington."

Malcolm's gaze narrowed. "And?"

"I can't tell if she knows something or not."

Mélanie slid her hand through her husband's arm and they gathered up Harry and Cordy and then followed Thomas into the antechamber, hung with a peacock-striped silk designed to complement many of Emily's gowns.

Charlotte Wilcox was sitting, back ramrod straight, on a striped satin settee across from the door. She pushed herself to her feet and came forwards quickly. She was a slender young woman with smooth ash brown hair, a level dark gaze, and a friendly smile. She wore ice blue net over satin with a much more demure neckline than Mélanie's gown or Cordy's silver gauze. Pearls gleamed at her throat and ears. The ensemble of a young woman not long out in society, but her gaze held the assurance of a woman with much more experience of life.

Thomas performed the necessary introductions, with propriety but without wasting time on unnecessary detail.

"Thank you all for coming," Miss Wilcox said. "I know it must seem as though we're being alarmist, but truly I can't think what happened."

"Miss Schofield didn't say anything to you before she disappeared that might be relevant?" Mélanie asked.

"You mean indicating that she might run off?" Miss Wilcox shook her head. A lock of brown hair slipped from its pins and swung beside her face. "That wasn't—isn't Marianne. She's brave, but she isn't the sort to run risks. If she felt she faced some sort of threat she'd have told someone."

"Do you have any reason to think she may have been under some sort of threat?" Malcolm asked.

Miss Wilcox's eyes widened. "You mean she might have been taken against her will?"

"It's one possibility. If you think it unlikely she ran off on her own, it's an even more likely possibility."

Miss Wilcox folded her arms over her chest. "Surely Mr. Thornsby talked to you."

"He did. But you've known Miss Schofield far longer."

Charlotte Wilcox frowned. Her brows were level and as direct as she seemed to be. "Marianne and I've been friends since we were in the nursery. We used to dream about making our debuts together."

"Was it as she expected?" Cordelia asked. "It's so exciting in the abstract, but the reality doesn't always live up to that."

Miss Wilcox's frown deepened. "You know the sort of dreams one has as a young girl. It wasn't precisely like that. But then it never is, is it?"

"I do think our dreams change as we get older," Mélanie said. "But a lot of girls are excited about their first season. Was Miss Schofield not?"

Miss Wilcox twisted her hands together against her net skirt, a seemingly uncharacteristic gesture. "There were a lot of expecta-tions. More than I have to face. Her mother, in particular, was determined Marianne would make a brilliant match. She had been for years. But when we were younger, I think it was easier for Marianne to see a brilliant match as the handsome prince of one's dreams. By the time one actually makes one's debut and meets young men—or not so young men—at Almack's and all the other coming-out balls, the reality can't but start to sink in."

"Was there someone else?" Malcolm asked.

"Someone else?" Miss Wilcox's dark eyes turned opaque.

"Someone else Miss Schofield cared about? Cares about?" Malcolm drew in his breath. Mélanie could feel him searching for the words. "Someone else she'd have preferred to marry."

"Oh no." Miss Wilcox said quickly. "I don't think Marianne really let herself think that way."

"She sounds singularly determined," Cordelia said. "It's difficult to control one's romantic impulses, particularly at eighteen."

"Marianne was very aware of her position in the world. She was never one to give in to her feelings easily."

"So you don't think she ran away with a lover?" Harry asked.

"No," Miss Wilcox said quickly. "That is—she'd never have put her family through an elopement."

"Sometimes it's the only option if a couple doesn't feel their parents will consent to the marriage," Cordy said.

"Yes, but Marianne wasn't—isn't—I'd have known if she was in love with someone."

"So you don't believe she was in love with Mr. Thornsby?" Harry asked. He glanced at Thomas, who was standing quietly beside them. "Forgive me. These are personal questions. But we need to understand to determine what may have become of her."

"She—" Miss Wilcox swallowed. Her gaze shot to Thomas.

"It's all right." Thomas's voice was tight and contained but not without sympathy. "They need to know whatever you understand. You knew—know—Marianne far better than I do."

Miss Wilcox met Thomas's gaze for a moment, then inclined her head. "I believe she esteemed Mr. Thornsby. She admired him. She thought they could be happy together."

"So she was happy in the betrothal?" Cordelia said.

"She—believed it was a prudent match."

Mélanie took a step forwards. "In my experience, no matter now sensible they are, people—especially young people—don't settle for prudent matches unless something has made them give up on love. What had made Miss Schofield do so?"

Miss Wilcox pleated a fold of her skirt. "Most of the men who sought Marianne out were blatant fortune hunters. She has a fortune, but the family is not—the family connections limited those who sought her out. Foolishly."

"I understand," Malcolm said in a quiet voice. "Our friend the current Lord Carfax's mother was in much the same situation."

Miss Wilcox met his gaze and nodded. "Mr. Thornsby—"

"Needed to marry a fortune," Thomas said. Bitterness cut through his tone like lye.

"You were quite honest about that," Miss Wilcox said. "Marianne said it was refreshing. And that she trusted you."

"That counts for a great deal." Mélanie cast a glance at Malcolm. "I wouldn't still be married to my husband if I didn't I trust him." Even though he'd been wrong to trust her at the start.

Miss Wilcox met her gaze for a moment. "Trust means a great deal. I believe Marianne thought—thinks—she could be happy with Mr. Thornsby." She looked at Thomas Thornsby for a moment. "It's a prudent match."

"That sounds like parents talking, not a young woman in her first season," Cordelia said.

"Marianne isn't a typical young woman in her first season."

"Tell us about your talk in the garden tonight," Malcolm said.

Miss Wilcox started. "What about it?"

"What did you discuss? How did Miss Schofield seem?"

Miss Wilcox's gloved fingers closed on her elbows. "Nothing in particular. We talked about how hot it was in the ballroom and how nice it was to breathe fresh air and how our dancing slippers were pinching. Marianne said she was tempted to see if a different style of shoe would be more comfortable. She asked me whom I was dancing with and I said—"

"It's quite understandable to be excited about dancing with one gentleman," Cordelia said. "Or to dread dancing with another."

Miss Wilcox's shoulders relaxed a trifle. "Marianne said that was one advantage to being betrothed. One didn't have to feel one had to dance every dance. But that all the fuss about the wedding was rather tiresome."

"We heard there was a bit of fuss about the mistletoe," Harry said.

"Oh." Miss Wilcox flushed. "Well, yes. Can you imagine anything more disagreeable than being asked to kiss someone in public?"

"It does seem quite horrid," Cordelia said with a smile, quite as if many of the incidents in her past didn't exist. "Was that part of the reason she wanted to leave the ballroom?"

"Perhaps. She didn't say so directly. But she did say she didn't like the notoriety an engagement brought and she didn't think Mr. Thornsby liked it either." Her gaze went to Thomas.

"No," Thomas said.

"It's not a pleasant way to share a first kiss," Cordelia said. "That is—"

"Oh yes," Miss Wilcox said. "I think it was their first kiss. Oh, that is—"

"Investigations often force one to share details one normally wouldn't dream of mentioning," Malcolm said.

"Is that what this is?" Miss Wilcox looked steadily at him. "An investigation?"

"Miss Schofield is missing, and we're trying to find her."

"So you think there's something wrong?"

"You and Mr. Thornsby evidently did. Or you wouldn't have come to us. I imagine it took a great deal to share your friend's predicament. You naturally wouldn't want to draw attention to it."

"It was a first kiss," Thomas said. "That is, it wasn't really a kiss at all."

Miss Wilcox swallowed. "I can't think why she would have left. If anyone is more cautious than I am, it's Marianne."

"Whom does she care for enough to run a risk?" Mélanie asked.

Miss Wilcox frowned. "She loves her family. But it's hard to imagine their being in trouble. Gerry and Sophy are practically still children, and Sally and Billy are in the schoolroom."

"Gerry's an undergraduate, isn't he?" Malcolm said.

"Yes." Miss Wilcox twisted her hands together. "Gerald is in his second year at Cambridge. Though he's been in town for a few weeks."

"Then he was here before the Michaelmas term ended," Malcolm said.

"Yes." Miss Wilcox smoothed a crease from her crumpled gloves. "Gerry—Gerald—came home early."

"He was sent down," Harry said.

Miss Wilcox glanced away, then met his gaze. "He was."

"Do you know why?" Malcolm asked.

"Why does that matter?"

"Because if her brother was in trouble, it could give Miss Schofield a motive to have run off."

"But Gerald was at the ball. Is at the ball."

"Does he know his sister is missing?" Mélanie asked.

"Good god, no. We—Mr. Thornsby and I—are doing everything in our power to keep Marianne's family from knowing."

"Why?" Malcolm asked.

"Why?" Miss Wilcox said on a note of disbelief.

"Yes. If my daughter were missing, my wife and I would want to know at once."

"Yes, but you're—you would know how to set about finding her. We don't want any scandal. Or disruption for the family."

"My wife and I know Gerald Schofield a bit," Harry said. "He's come to Classicists' Society events. I believe he introduced his sister to Thornsby."

"He did," Thomas said.

Harry nodded. "But I can't claim to be in his confidence. Does either of you know why he was sent down?"

Miss Wilcox pressed her finger over another wrinkle in her

glove. "I don't know the whole of it. Even with me Marianne is circumspect." She looked at Thomas.

"She was even more circumspect with me," Thomas said. "If she confided in anyone, it was you. Please share what you know. They need all the information we have to give."

Miss Wilcox nodded. "But I believe there were gambling debts involved. And from something Marianne said, I think it may also have concerned a woman."

"A woman at Cambridge?" Harry said.

"Why should that matter?"

Harry leaned forwards, leg dangling against the fluted leg of the table he'd perched on. "Because if the woman came to see Miss Schofield or sent her a message, that might be one way to account for her leaving. Easier for the woman to do that in London. Though of course if she's from Cambridge, she could have traveled to London."

"But surely—you think this woman broke into a ball?"

"Miss Schofield evidently left a ball without attracting notice."

Miss Wilcox drew in and released her breath, tugging at the draped shoulders of her gown and making the silk rosettes at the neck flutter. "I can't see Marianne leaving with a woman she didn't even know."

"Even if the woman claimed to be able to hurt Miss Schofield's brother?" Cordelia said. "Or to be with child by him?"

Miss Wilcox's gaze snapped to Cordy's face. "You can't know—"

"Of course not," Cordelia said. "But it's one possible outcome of an unfortunate entanglement. One that could put a young woman in a desperate situation where she might well seek out the young man. There was evidently something bad enough to cause young Mr. Schofield to be sent down."

Miss Wilcox regraded Cordelia as though she were some sort of exotic animal, equally hypnotic and dangerous. "Marianne would have wanted to protect Gerry. But she wasn't—isn't—blind to his—to his faults. She'd also have wanted to help anyone she thought might have been hurt by him."

"So if the woman he'd been involved with had approached her or sent her a note—" Cordelia said.

Miss Wilcox drew in and released her breath. "If she had sought Marianne out and asked for help, or sent Marianne a note asking Marianne to meet her, Marianne might have left Lady Cowper's. That's one of the few reasons I can see that she might have done so. Assuming this woman exists at all. Assuming she's the reason Gerry was sent down. And that she somehow got into Lady Cowper's garden."

"Whoever may have got into the garden," Mélanie said, "Marianne Schofield somehow managed to get out. Without anyone's knowing."

Miss Wilcox rubbed her arms. "That's the oddest thing. I still can't figure out how Marianne left."

"Through the garden gate and the mews, presumably," Malcolm said.

Miss Wilcox stared at him. She was very free of missish airs. But the thought of a friend going in her ball dress through the gate to the cobbled mews where the horses and tack were kept, walking in the shadows over manure in satin dancing slippers, seemed to be unthinkable.

"When faced with improbable options, one settles on the least impossible," Malcolm said.

Miss Wilcox nodded. "So she must have very much wanted to leave." She looked at Thomas. "And not felt she could turn to either of us for help."

CHAPTER 8

$\mathcal{A}$ French window clicked shut. Footsteps pattered over the terrace cobblestones. A young woman was running from the house, her gauzy white gown bright in the shadows. For a moment Kitty wondered if it might be Marianne Schofield, until the moonlight caught the woman's dark hair.

The young woman came to a skidding stop on the edge of the terrace above where Laura, Raoul, Kitty, and Julien were standing. "Oh, sorry." She teetered on the damp stones. "I was looking for my sister."

Julien reached up a hand to steady her. "Is your sister Marianne Schofield?"

"Yes, do you know her?" The young woman gripped his proffered hand without alarm or embarrassment.

"Not precisely," Laura said. "We know her fiancé, Thomas Thornsby."

"Oh." The young woman released Julien's hand and plopped down on the stone wall at the edge of the terrace. "I'm Sophia Schofield. Sophy. I know one isn't supposed to introduce oneself, but you already know I'm Marianne's sister, and those rules are rot."

"I couldn't agree more," Julien said. "I'm Julien Mallinson. My wife Kitty. And Laura and Raoul O'Roarke."

"Pleased to meet you." Sophy Schofield frowned. "Wait a minute, aren't you Lord Carfax?"

"I try to forget it whenever possible. But yes, rather regrettably, I am."

"Oh, well. If Mama fusses, I'll tell her I met an earl and countess. And you're talked about everywhere." She looked from Julien and Kitty to Laura and Raoul. "And you all investigate things, don't you?"

"At times," Raoul said.

"Is that why you're here tonight?" Sophy Schofield leaned back, braced on her hands with a fine disregard for her gloves. "I wish someone would tell me what's going on tonight. It's quite plain there are dark doings afoot with Charlotte and Mr. Thornsby huddled together behind branches of pine and holly. And not in the way ladies and gentleman generally do at a ball. Which would certainly be awkward in their case. Not that Marianne would have noticed, I haven't seen her for hours." She scanned their faces. "I'd think Marianne had run off, except that she's far too well-bred to do anything so dashing. Or so sensible."

"You don't think your sister is sensible?" Laura said.

"That depends on what you mean by sensible. Most people would say she is. Marianne's always been perfect. She always does exactly what's expected of her. Of course, it helps that she always does it perfectly." Sophy stuck her legs out and frowned at the pink silk rosettes on her slippers. "She plays the piano beautifully. She sings perfectly. I sound like a cat howling. She paints perfect watercolors. Mine are smudges. She pours tea and passes the cups round without splashing even a drop in the saucer. She knows all the steps of the waltz and the boulanger and the quadrille and goodness knows how many country dances, and she curtsies as though she's dancing. She knows which tippet goes with which gown and which bonnet will set off which spencer, and how to keep a shawl draped perfectly over her arms instead of getting hopelessly tangled and slithering to the floor. And she seems to *like* all of it. She likes planning her outfits and changing them four times a day. She enjoys the parties, even if she's nervous about them. It's like she can't imagine anyone's not enjoying that life. And of course Mama likes it. Marianne is just the sort of daughter she wanted. Marianne always has been. I never have. That's why she thought I should have a quiet debut in the little season instead of waiting for next spring. Even so, I don't think Mama thought I'd be such a complete and utter disappointment when it came to having my season."

"I wouldn't assume that," Kitty said. "I lost my mother when I was quite young, and I don't think I was ever the sort of daughter she expected, but I don't think I disappointed her."

Laura cast a quick glance at Kitty. Her words had been a rare admission, Kitty realized. She almost never talked about her parents.

"Yes," Sophy said, "but you look as though—you obviously understand the rules of the game."

"And you don't?" Kitty asked.

"No, I do, but I think they're silly."

"Well, that's a point," Kitty said. "I do too."

"But you follow them anyway?"

"Not precisely. " Kitty smoothed her hands over the ruffles that ran down the front of her gold satin gown and looked steadily at Sophy. "I learned the rules because sometimes I think they matter to my husband."

"So you did it to make your husband happy." Sophy's lips curled.

Julien snorted.

Kitty cast a look at him. "Oh no. My husband thinks the rules are silly. And he'd be horrified at the thought that I gave any heed to them, let alone that I did so for reasons having anything remotely to do with him. But he has some rather good ideas that could help make the world a better place. And he has a better chance of working for them if we aren't complete social outcasts."

Sophy frowned. "That's a better reason than I can think of for going along with any of it." She looked from Kitty to Julien. "I suppose you're madly in love."

Kitty smiled. "You could put it that way." Out of the corner of her eye, she could see the glint in Julien's eyes. A year ago, neither of them would have even used the word though they'd been more or less living together.

"That's another good reason. I thought that was part of why Marianne was going along with it all, to be honest. That she wanted to meet the right man and fall madly in love and be happy. Not that it makes any sense to me that meeting the right man would automatically make one happy and content with every-thing that should logically make a person discontented, but if Marianne thought it would work for her, I could sort of under-stand it."

"But you didn't think she was in love with Mr. Thornsby?" Laura asked.

"Good god, no. Have you seen the way they look at each other? Well, perhaps you haven't noticed. There's nothing remarkable about the way they look at each other. That's the whole point. I'm hardly an expert on romance—I tend to think it's vastly overrated —but I do know people in love tend to look at each other in a sickening way."

"Perhaps your sister thinks romance is overrated as well," Laura suggested.

Sophy frowned. "It's true she never seemed the romantic sort. But while I think love is silly and I can't imagine giving up—well, everything one gives up to get married—just for a man—I can sort of imagine thinking it worthwhile if one were madly in love. At least, thinking it worthwhile long enough to get married and repent later."

"But it sounds like your sister values different things from you," Kitty said.

"She does. I never realized how much until she became betrothed. It was quite obvious she hadn't been holding out for falling madly in love. Because it couldn't have been more obvious she and Mr. Thornsby weren't in love."

"You don't care for Mr. Thornsby?" Julien asked.

"Oh, no, I quite like him. He's sensible, and he tells fascinating stories about Roman history that I don't think Mama would approve of at all if she knew about them. But he doesn't seem to have the least bit in common with Marianne. I mean, it's his classical studies that make him interesting, and Marianne doesn't seem to care about them. And if she wants to be a great lady and cut dash in society, I don't think he's the right husband for her at all."

"That's very true," Laura said.

Sophy looked among them. "So what on earth is going on? Do they want to call it off? Are they trying to come up with an explanation? I could almost believe that, except that it's hard to see Marianne's doing anything so disruptive as crying off from a betrothal. But perhaps Mr. Thornsby wants to?" Her face brightened.

"I can't imagine Thornsby's crying off from a betrothal," Raoul said. "He would agree that that is strictly the lady's prerogative."

"Poison." Sophy crossed her arms over her chest. "What on earth are he and Charlotte so busy talking about then? And where is Marianne?" She looked among them. "Good god, is that it? Is Marianne missing? What's happened?"

Laura cast a quick look at her husband and then Kitty and Julien. "When did you last see your sister?"

Sophy frowned. "When we made up a set with Reggie Patterson and Tim Barnett. I caught my heel in my flounce and almost went skidding down on the floorboards. Reggie just looked clueless and started to tumble after me. Marianne saved me from falling and then we both grabbed Reggie and somehow, thanks to Marianne, we all actually managed to go on with the set. After that, I had to dance another dance with Reggie, and she went off to talk to Charlotte. I saw them go out in the garden. That's one advantage of being betrothed. You can not dance every dance and no one thinks you're a wallflower."

"That fits," Raoul said. "We know she went into the garden."

"Where did she go next?"

"We aren't sure. No one appears to have seen her after Miss Wilcox went back inside."

"But—do Mama and Papa know?"

"Not yet," Raoul said. "Mr. Thornsby and Miss Wilcox were most desirous of their not knowing."

"Yes, I can quite see that. They'd only fuss and make it harder to keep secret. And even I can quite see not wanting a scandal."

"Is this your sister's earring?" Raoul held out the pink earring they'd found.

Sophy studied it in the light from the lanterns. "No. Marianne was wearing moonstones tonight."

"Interesting." Raoul pocketed the earring. "Your sister must not have been the only lady to seek refuge in the garden tonight."

"Can you think of anyone your sister would have left to help?" Laura asked.

"No. I mean, Marianne's kindhearted, but she's not a risk-taker. And most everyone she cares about is here. Well, except for the children. Billy and Sally. Our little brother and sister."

"They're home?" Raoul said.

"Yes. Sally was grumbling about being in the schoolroom and Billy was saying he was lucky he didn't have to go to boring balls."

"Do you think we could talk to them?" Raoul asked.

Sophy stared at him. "You mean, go to our house?"

"If you wouldn't mind taking us," Raoul said.

"Not that we aren't quite capable of breaking in," Laura said, "but we wouldn't want to frighten your brother and sister."

"They're not the sort to frighten, but—" Sophy's eyes widened. "Are you asking me to sneak out of the ball as well?"

"If you wouldn't mind," Raoul said.

A smile lit Sophy's face. "That's the most exciting offer I've had all season."

CHAPTER 9

"Mélanie!" Lucinda Mallinson caught Mélanie's arm. "What's going on?"

Mélanie, who had just emerged from their interview with Charlotte Wilcox, steadied herself under the grip of Hubert Mallinson's youngest child. "Why should anything be going on? Besides the holidays, Emily's ball, and everyone still talking about the queen's case."

"You know what I mean." Lucinda lowered her voice and dragged Mélanie into an alcove created by a statue of Aphrodite and a vase of pine boughs tied with red velvet ribbon. "If you and Malcolm are here—not to mention Laura and Raoul, and Cordy and Harry, and Kitty and Julien—something is obviously going on. I know I shouldn't pry, but is it to do with Marianne Schofield?"

Mélanie studied the younger woman. Lucinda was clever, but that was quick even for her. "What makes you ask that?"

"Well, obviously I noticed she's disappeared."

Mélanie shifted her shoulders so her back was to the passage and her voice pitched for Lucinda alone. "When did you notice that?"

"I'm not blind, Mélanie. I realized over an hour ago that I hadn't seen Marianne for ages, so I started looking round for her. I mean, I couldn't help but be concerned."

"Why? I mean, why were you particularly concerned about Miss Schofield? It's not uncommon to lose sight of someone at a ball."

"Mélanie." Lucinda fixed Mélanie with a level blue gaze that suddenly put Mélanie in mind of Hubert Mallinson. "I'm not an idiot. It's obvious Marianne isn't happy about her betrothal to Thomas Thornsby."

"I didn't know you knew Miss Schofield so well." Mélanie had always been fond of Lucinda, but though they worked with Hubert Mallinson surprisingly often, they were hardly social intimates of the family. And these days they went out in society less.

"We made our debuts together," Lucinda said. "One sees those girls at all the same parties and at Almack's and all sorts of other places that sound much more exciting in theory than they are in fact. At the Duchess of Trenchard's ball, Marianne and I both took refuge on the balcony and got to talking, and I realized she was much more sensible than most of the other girls in their first season. Or she was more sensible about being in her first season. And then her friend Charlotte Wilcox came out onto the balcony as well and I realized Charlotte was sensible too. Ever since that, I've seen the two of them as a refuge."

"Did Miss Schofield tell you she didn't want to marry Thomas Thornsby?"

"Well, no. Not in so many words." Lucinda dragged the cream satin toe of her dancing slipper over Emily Cowper's polished floorboards. "She smiled when she told me about it, but it was one of *those* smiles. You know. The sort Mama gives when she says she's delighted to see someone and I know perfectly well she's been hoping to avoid them. The sort Malcolm gives at parties, when I know he'd rather be in the library. Or that David gives when someone tells him he's sure to find the right girl this season.

I expect it's the sort of smile Papa gives when he orders a difficult agent killed. Not that I see that."

"So it was a smile that hides the truth."

"Yes, precisely. Which is odd, because for all she's reserved, Marianne was usually honest with me and with Charlotte. That was the core of our friendship. That we were honest with each other."

"Did she tell Miss Wilcox about her betrothal at the same time?"

"Yes, it was at the Esterhazys', just after she'd accepted Mr. Thornsby. She said she wanted to tell us first. She had the most fixed look on her face, like she was a figure in wax. I just stared at her because it seemed so odd. Then Charlotte squeezed her hand and said this was splendid news, Mr. Thornsby was such a kind man, and she knew this was just what Marianne had wanted."

"What did Miss Schofield say?"

"She said, 'So you wish me happy?' And Charlotte said, 'Of course I do.' And then there was this sort of awkward silence, and I realized I had to say I wished her happy too, which I did, but I've never felt as though I was lying to Marianne before. It felt rather like a betrayal of our friendship. And Marianne seemed to know how I felt because the silence just got more awkward, and she gave this rather tight smile and said she knew it was the right thing to do."

"Why do you think she accepted Thomas Thornsby?"

Lucinda wrinkled her nose. "Her parents wanted her to find a husband. Well, I suppose mine do. I mean, Mama does. I don't think Papa worries about it so much. In fact, one night when we came back from a ball and Mama was fussing about whom I'd danced with, Papa stopped me on the way to his study after Mama went up, and said not to worry about what people wanted me to do. That surprised me. He didn't used to even pay enough attention to any of us to notice something like that. I think perhaps it was because of Louisa." She twisted her hands in her crimsonsprigged skirt at the reference to her late sister. Not for the first time, Mélanie wondered how much Lucinda knew about Louisa's life and death. Hopefully not the full truth.

Lucinda drew a breath and released the folds of her skirt. "I have a comfortable fortune, of course. I needn't marry if I don't want to. I'm not sure that would have been the case if Papa had never been Lord Carfax, but I know Julien saw to it we were all provided for when he and Papa settled everything. Which was rather decent of him, considering what I think Papa did to him. It gives me choices in life."

"Miss Schofield is an heiress. She shouldn't need to marry either, if she doesn't want to."

"Oh, yes. She has more of a fortune than I do, though I don't like thinking about such things. But her parents—I mean, Mama wants me to marry, but I can't imagine her compelling me to."

"And you think Miss Schofield's parents were compelling her to marry Mr. Thornsby?"

"No. Not precisely. I mean, they weren't locking her up or feeding her bread and water or anything. But she knew how much it mattered to them. She didn't want to disappoint them. That can be a compulsion of a sort."

"It certainly can."

"I even said it to her. Not that night. I was too startled and confused to know how to respond. I knew Marianne would prob- ably marry, but I expected her to fall in love, and it was quite clear she wasn't in love with Mr. Thornsby. She didn't even pretend to be. So when I saw her at the Tavistock the next night—at the new *Hamlet*—I pulled her aside in the grand salon and said was it really worth it making herself unhappy just to please her parents. And Marianne looked at me as though I were sickening with some- thing and said she wasn't in the least unhappy. It was harder to talk after that. She didn't avoid me, but things weren't as easy between us. I asked Charlotte if we should do something, and Charlotte said we couldn't. I had the oddest sense she knew something I didn't. But she wouldn't talk about it more. She said Marianne would be happy." Lucinda looked at Mélanie with wide eyes. Suddenly she seemed closer to Colin and Jessica's age. "You don't think I caused Marianne to run somehow, do you? By asking questions?"

"I very much doubt it, Lucy. And if she ran off because she's unhappy and you had something to do with making her realize she was unhappy, I'm not sure that's a bad thing."

"Truly?"

"Compared to going into a marriage that would make her miserable?"

"I suppose—yes, I can see that. But what if she's in danger?"

"We have no reason to believe she is," Mélanie said. Though she felt far less sanguine than this sounded.

Lucinda's gaze said she sensed Mélanie's doubts. "I knew. About Mr. Thornsby and Edith. Or I guessed. But I couldn't say that to Marianne. It seemed wrong to talk to her about it somehow. I can't quite articulate why—I mean, one doesn't want to tell someone their betrothed may love someone else. Even if they don't love their betrothed. And yet, I can't help but think she should know."

"Perhaps she does already."

"And that's why she ran off?" Lucinda frowned. "I admit I've thought some quite uncharitable things about Mr. Thornsby for not simply marrying Edith. But I know the family are in difficult straits. I've never had to even think about fortune or the lack of it in that way. For all Mama complained when we left Carfax House —which just meant leaving a very large house for a slightly less large one. And even she's never told me I had to marry for money. I think that's a beastly expectation for girls, but for boys too."

"Yes," Mélanie said.

"I don't suppose you ever—oh, of course, you were in the midst of a war when you married."

"Among other things." Like spying on her husband. "A lot of people assume I married Malcolm for his money."

"But you didn't," Lucinda said, as though stating that the moon would rise.

"I was penniless when he married me. I couldn't quite grasp the scale he lived on."

"Yes, but you didn't marry him *because* of that. Can you imagine marrying for money?"

"I can imagine all sorts of things under the right circumstances." After all, she'd certainly married Malcolm for advantage, even if it was more tactical than financial.

Lucinda wrinkled her nose. "I keep thinking Edith and Mr. Thornsby should simply run off together."

"I find myself thinking that too."

"That's what would happen in a novel. But then the novel would just be over. And one always assumes the hero and heroine will be happy, because—well, one wants to think that."

"Quite," Mélanie said. She could admit that to Lucinda. Far more easily than she could to her husband or friends of her own age.

"But if Edith and Mr. Thornsby ran off together, I'm not sure they'd be happy," Lucinda said.

"Nor am I." Though Mélanie found herself wanting to believe it. With what the most detached part of her called naiveté.

"Still," Lucinda said, "it seems they should have the chance to sort that out for themselves. And Marianne shouldn't have to be in the middle of it."

"I quite agree."

"So you'll find her?"

"We're all doing our best to do so."

"I should let you get on with it. But please let me help if I can."

"Of course." Mélanie turned to go, then looked back over her shoulder. "Lucy? Is there anything else you know about Marianne that might help us?"

"What?" Lucinda started. "No, of course not. I'd have told you."

"All right. But if you think of anything, anything at all, let me know." Mélanie slipped from behind the pine branches. One tangled with a strand of her hair. The perils of leaving it down. She pulled it free, tugging more than she should have done. She'd known Lucinda for six years. She'd watched her grow up and listened to confidences she doubted Lucinda had shared with her parents.

And she was quite sure this was the first time Hubert Mallinson's forthright youngest child had ever lied to her.

CHAPTER 10

homas looked at Harry as they negotiated the passage outside the antechamber in which they had spoken with Charlotte Wilcox. "You must despise me."

Harry turned to regard his friend. "My dear fellow. Of course not. I wish you and Miss Schofield very happy."

"But you don't expect we will be."

"I'd never presume to know what marriage will be successful. Or what makes anyone else happy."

Thomas glanced away. "Having heard what you've heard tonight, can you honestly say you think we'll be happy?"

"I can say I don't think you're in love. Neither of you makes any pretensions to it. But then, I was desperately in love with Cordy when we married, and I was thoroughly miserable for the first year we were together—and the subsequent years we were apart."

"But you aren't miserable now."

"No, quite the opposite. But I don't think one counts on things working out as they did for us. I wouldn't say love is any guarantee of happiness. Though being in love with someone else can be a burden."

Thomas drew a hard breath.

Harry paused for a moment. "Does Miss Schofield know?"

"What?"

"About Edith."

"Good God." Thomas's head swung round. "You can't think I'd tell her."

"It seems to be a pertinent part of what will be the foundation of your marriage."

Thomas swallowed. "She knows I can't offer my heart. I don't believe she wishes me to do so. She doesn't know more. It all seemed workable. A few days ago. Now—" He stared at an oil of a bewitching eighteen-year-old Emily Cowper (when she had been Emily Lamb) that hung on the passage wall. "I wonder how I could have been such a fool."

Harry clapped a hand on his shoulder. "We're all fools, in love."

"But I'm not in love with Marianne."

"Precisely."

Thomas turned to look at him. His gaze was suddenly that of an anguished schoolboy. "If you and Lady Cordelia had never mended things—would you rather have been comfortably married to someone you esteemed but didn't love?"

Harry's mind shot back to the past. Especially to those days when his marriage had seemed to be in ashes. "It's a bit different. I didn't have dependants to think about. I had the luxury of wallowing in self-absorption. But—no. As I wrote to Cordelia the night before Waterloo, if I'd died in the battle, the time we had together would still have been worth it. Whatever the pain, I'd have been forever grateful for it. I still am."

"ANYTHING WRONG?" Julien drew Mélanie to the side, behind a statue of Juno draped in dark green fabric and wearing a holly crown, and scanned her face.

"I was talking to Lucinda. She's worried about Marianne Schofield. They were friends. Closer friends than I'd realized. She knew Marianne wasn't in love with Thomas Thornsby. She knows Thomas is in love with Edith. With all the fervor of the young, she wants to believe Thomas and Edith could run off together and be happy. And I confess I agree with her more than I would ever admit to my more rational and mature friends."

"Not surprising."

Mélanie shot a look at him. "You're the first I'd have thought would mock me for the least hint of romanticism."

"My dear. I'm far too prey to it myself."

Mélanie folded her arms and leaned back against the fluted paneling. "Julien, you didn't even admit you believed in love until less than a year ago."

"And then I believed Kitty and I could marry and be happy. What else do you call that?"

Mélanie choked. "You were right."

"That's only because Kitty is so amazing. But I don't think anyone would call it a rational belief."

"Define rational."

He grinned. "Precisely."

"Next you'll be saying you'd like Thomas and Edith to run off together."

"Of course I would." Julien gave a sheepish smile when she frowned at him in disbelief. "Nothing like being madly in love to make one want everyone to feel the same."

"Even if there's no guarantee it will work?"

"There's never a guarantee. Say what you will about love, it's always an adventure."

"Of course we're cushioned on the adventure."

"Quite. A comfortable fortune cushions all sorts of risks. Kitty and I could live in Carfax House and never see each other if we decided we couldn't bear the sight of each other."

"It's not the only path to happiness."

"I thought you didn't believe in happiness." He met her gaze, her comrade from their adventures with Hortense Bonaparte nine years ago. Her own words on a stream bank in Switzerland echoed in her head.

"I thought you didn't either."

"I never really admitted it even existed." An odd look crossed his face. "It seemed like a fairy tale. One more fairy tale to add to the rest of the ones you and O'Roarke believed in."

"And yet I don't think you entirely didn't believe. If you didn't believe in happiness, why would you have helped the people who took the *Unicorn* achieve it?"

"That was freedom. Which I suppose one could say is essential to happiness."

"Which seems prosaic."

"Nothing wrong with the prosaic. We're talking about a happiness one can achieve at every level of society. Though it's a bit easier with food and a roof over one's head."

"But even if we agree about happiness—*sacrebleu*, are the two of us really having this conversation?—marriage doesn't equal happiness for everyone."

"No. They'll have to sort that out for themselves. They just deserve the chance to do so."

"I don't think Thomas will give himself a chance to do anything until we find Miss Schofield." The last moments of her talk with Lucinda drifted through Mélanie's mind.

"What is it?" Julien asked.

"Nothing. Or perhaps nothing. But I have the oddest sense Lucinda wasn't telling me everything she knows about Miss Schofield."

"Not surprising, perhaps. Friends keep confidences. And we're practically the older generation. We may be cousins, but I'm old enough to be her father."

"Yes, but Lucinda was obviously worried about Marianne.

You'd think she'd trust us to find her. It's difficult to imagine what secrets she might feel she couldn't share with me."

"Perhaps she made a promise to Miss Schofield to keep her confidence."

"Perhaps. But Lucy has her father's ruthless pragmatism. I'm quite sure if she thought it was important enough, she'd tell us, and confidences be damned. Which means whatever it is, she's worried about the consequences of sharing it with us."

CHAPTER 11

"*D*avenport. Oh, I don't suppose you remember me. I'm—"

"Gerald Schofield." Harry turned to greet Marianne's younger brother. He and Thomas had just parted ways in the passage. "You came to my last Classicists' Society lecture."

"Yes! It was splendid. Never saw Claudius's regime in quite that way. Makes one want to see what he could have done with more time."

"Yes, my thoughts as well. Are you reading classics?"

"Oh, yes. Not that I have much pretension to—much of anything. Though I do contribute to the Cambridge Forum."

"I'm an Oxonian, but they put out some impressive papers."

"A lot of it's pretentious undergraduate sort of blather—I'm an undergraduate, and I can see that."

"There was a series of papers by an H. Hawkins lately that were quite impressive."

Schofield's gaze brightened. "You liked those? I thought they were splendid."

"I'd like to meet the writer. If he's a friend of yours, you should bring him along to the Classicists' Society."

"Oh, I'd—that would be splendid, sir. Thank you." Young Schofield smiled, but a look of uncertainty crossed his face. "I'll see if I can make that happen. Very good of you."

"The Classicists' Society need new ideas. And Hawkins is particularly original."

"He is that. Wish I could write—and think—half so well." Gerry cast a glance round the passage. "I say, have you seen Thornsby? I'm looking for him."

"Yes, I was just talking to him. I'm not sure where he's got to. May I presume you want to find him because you're concerned about your sister?"

Gerry's eyes widened. "What makes you think—?"

"Because Thornsby asked for my and my friends' help on your sister's account." Harry jerked his head towards a door across the passage, which he profoundly hoped opened onto an antechamber. "In here."

The door did indeed open onto an antechamber hung with slightly faded yellow-flowered silk. Gerry Schofield stalked across the room and faced Harry. He had dark hair cut into what was obviously an attempt at a Byronic crop. His hair flopped over his forehead, somehow making his round, well-scrubbed face look all the more schoolboyish.

"What's happened to my sister?" he demanded.

"How do you know anything's happened?" Harry asked.

Young Schofield pushed the floppy lock of hair back from his forehead. "I'm not an idiot, Davenport. Marianne hasn't been in the ballroom for well over an hour. I walked through the other rooms and couldn't see her. I'm not the sort of brother who hovers, but I do notice my sisters. It was already obvious something was wrong. And then you immediately knew I was worried about Marianne. That makes it clear."

"Sound reasoning."

"I told you I'm not an idiot." Gerry took a step forwards. "What's happened to Marianne?"

"We don't know.," Harry said. "She was in the garden with her friend Miss Wilcox—"

"Charlotte."

"Yes. And she seems to have disappeared from there."

"With someone?"

"We don't know. Can you think of anyone who would have come to talk to her?"

"Why on earth should I be able to think of anyone?"

Harry pulled a straight-backed chair forwards and sat. "Can you think of anyone connected to you who might have sought your sister out?"

"Why should anyone connected to me have sought Marianne out?" Gerry dropped onto the sofa across from Harry. "Except family, and they're connected to both of us."

"You came down from Cambridge recently," Harry said

Schofield flushed, but didn't look away. "Was sent down, you mean."

"Another word for it."

"Got into a bit of trouble over gaming debts."

"So did a number of my friends in our university days. It usually wasn't enough to get sent down."

Gerry studied the toes of his shoes. "Perhaps my problems were worse than your friends'."

"Perhaps. There wasn't a woman involved?"

Gerry's gaze shot to Harry's face. "What have you heard?"

"Let's say we've heard rumors."

"Damn it, no one should have known—"

"Regardless of who knew what, might the woman involved have sought out your sister?"

"What? No! Justine would have had no reason to seek out Marianne."

"Is Justine angry at you?"

"No!" Gerry's hand froze as he dug his fingers into his hair again. "That is, I hope not."

"Is there any chance she's with child?"

"With—? Good god, no. It's not like that."

"It's a common consequence of such entanglements."

"But we weren't—Justine's father is a tutor at Cambridge."

That was not what one would normally think of for a liaison at university, but Harry had known of other undergraduates entangled with tutors' daughters. "Her father was your tutor?" he asked.

"Yes, that's how we'd met. Well, our fathers were at Cambridge together themselves, but we didn't see each other much growing up. Then her father become my tutor, and we'd talk after my lessons. That was how it started."

"How you became involved."

"Yes. No. That was when she first gave me the papers."

"Papers?"

"Yes. Justine's quite brilliant at classics. Much more than I am, but it gave us something to talk about. She showed me some papers she'd written. They were better than anything I've seen in the Forum. Better than anything I've written for the Forum. And it seemed so bloody unfair that Justine's papers couldn't be in the Forum just because she couldn't go to university. Well, actually it seemed bloody unfair she couldn't go to Cambridge. But I couldn't fix that."

"But you could get her papers published," Harry said.

Gerry nodded. "At first Justine wanted me to publish them under my name, but I said that wasn't fair. I wouldn't take credit for something I couldn't have written myself. So we made up a name. And it worked fine for the first one. But Hopkins—he's the editor of the Forum and he was considered the best writer until Justine's articles—got suspicious. He started poking round and asking questions. So I vouched that I knew Humphrey Hawkins—that's the name we made up."

"As I told you, I was impressed," Harry said. "A lot of nuance and a masterful understanding of language and first-century culture."

"Yes, isn't she amazing?" Gerry's face shone with pride and admiration. "But after I vouched for Humphrey Hawkins, the next thing I knew I was accused of aiding plagiarism and fraud. And they wanted me to say who wrote the articles, and of course I couldn't because that would have meant getting Justine in trouble and probably her father, who didn't know anything about it. Justine wanted to come forwards, but I pointed out that would get her father in trouble. He's a private tutor, dependent on the students who engage his services, so any sort of scandal could lose him money. And I was much better able to deal with being sent down than he was with losing private tutoring students. It quite lends a fellow a bit of caché to be sent down. Not that I really wanted that sort of caché."

"So there were no gambling debts?" Harry said.

"What? Oh, no. I just tried to put that about to explain why I was sent down, so no one would suspect about Justine and her father. But I don't see how this could have anything to do with Marianne."

"She didn't know about it?" Harry said.

"No. She asked me if I wanted to talk about it—about my being sent down—but I said there wasn't anything to say. No sense burdening her with that, with everything else going on."

"Everything else?" Harry said.

"I mean the betrothal. They met because of me." Gerry scraped a hand over his hair. "Always liked Thornsby. He took pains to welcome me at the Classicists' Society. Listened to me with far more patience than I had any right to expect. Still remember how shocked I was when I saw him at Almack's. I mean, one gets used to seeing people in a certain setting. Even though you know that you live in the same city and your families move in the same circles."

"I quite understand," Harry said. Like seeing fellow agents at a family engagement. Though at this point, most of his family were agents, however one defined family.

"In any case," Gerry said, "there he was at Almack's, and it was splendid to see someone I could have rational conversation with. That is—"

"I quite understand," Harry said. "Most people aren't at Almack's for rational conversation."

"So of course I introduced him to my sisters and he introduced me to his. And of course we asked them to dance. That's the polite thing to do at Almack's. I was quite pleased to see him and Marianne getting on. Then the next day he called. I think it was to talk to me actually, but of course Marianne was there. And we met him walking in the park the day after, and they got to talking again. He's a very decent fellow. Just what one wants for one's sister. But—"

Harry watched him in silence as his voice trailed off.

Gerry scraped the shiny black toe of his dress shoe over the carpet. "Can't claim to be an expert on what makes two people happy. But it was plain to me that neither of their—er—hearts were engaged. I know that probably sounds fulsome, but—"

"It sounds insightful," Harry said.

Gerry met his gaze. "I kept thinking I was missing something. And I might have simply put it down to that. But—well—I'd been to the Classicists' Society."

"And you'd seen Thornsby and Miss Simmons."

"Er—yes." Gerry glanced to the side. "Can't claim to be an expert on such things. And they're always perfectly correct with each other. But I could hardly fail to notice—that is, I may have been imagining it, but—"

"No." Harry said. "And Thornsby himself is too honest to claim you were imagining it."

"Well, then."

"There are reasons why Thornsby and Miss Simmons don't think they can marry."

"Fortune." Gerry's gaze locked on Harry's own, unexpectedly hard.

"Primarily."

"And Marianne's an heiress. And my parents want a title."

"Do you think your sister doesn't realize that?"

Gerry dragged his toe over the carpet again. "No. That is, I think she realized it. Well, I know she did. I tried to talk to her. After the betrothal. I asked her if this was what she really wanted. And she said of course it was, and she'd have thought I'd be happy, Thornsby was a friend of mine. I said Thornsby was capital but it was plain they weren't in love. She looked at me in that pitying way that makes it seem as though she's the one who's older, and said most marriages weren't about love, they were bargains, and she and Thornsby knew what they were getting and were making a good bargain. I said she didn't have to make a choice just because it was what Mother and Father wanted. "

"What did she say to that?" Harry asked.

Gerry frowned. "That there weren't any other options for her, so this was a sensible choice and she might as well make them happy. Which was nonsense. I mean, she's a pretty girl with a handsome fortune and there are heaps of chaps about. Surely if she waited a few years she'd fall in love with one of them."

"So you have no reason to think she'd have run off?"

"Run off?" Gerry shook his head as though Harry had suggested Marianne had gone to the moon. "No. Marianne was very set on proceeding with her betrothal. Not like anyone was pushing her into it or anything."

"And there was nothing she was afraid of?"

"Afraid? Marianne? I mean, we live ridiculously sheltered lives, as I suppose the Radicals would say. Nothing for any of us to worry about. And Marianne's far too level-headed to be afraid."

"Anyone she would leave to help?"

Gerry's brows knotted tighter. "The family're all here. Well, all but Sally and Billy."

"Sally and Billy?" Harry asked.

"Our little brother and sister. In the nursery. Well, the schoolroom anyway. Wouldn't thank me for calling them the Infantry. But still. Can't imagine how they could be in trouble. And while they get up to mischief, can't see their calling Marianne away. The rest of us are here. And Charlotte. And Charlotte would never get into trouble any more than Marianne would. They were both always sensible, even in the schoolroom. That's what's so odd about this. If Sophy—our sister—disappeared, I could give you ten possible scenarios without even drawing breath. And I suppose they might even do the same for me. But no one expects Marianne to do anything except—well, be perfect."

CHAPTER 12

"Are we going to climb the walls?" Sophy asked as she stopped before the front steps of her parents' house two streets over from Emily Cowper's in George Street. Not a long walk, but Laura had had time to feel pang for the cloak she'd relinquished to Emily's footman. She could feel the damp December chill through the thin silk and cashmere of her shawl and the velvet of her gown.

"Nothing so dramatic," Raoul said. "We'll use the area door."

Sophy frowned. "I think the servants lock it at this hour."

"No need to worry. I should be able to manage the lock."

Sophy's eyes widened. Raoul didn't add that he could also manage to scale the walls. He'd climbed the walls to visit Laura in her bedchamber more than once before they were married. Marriage did take away some of the adventure of life. Though with Raoul, a healthy share of adventure of all sorts would always remain.

Sophy led the way down the area steps. Raoul picked the lock with one of Laura's hairpins while Laura and Sophy provided cover. Sophy let out a whistle of appreciation when the lock clicked open. "Can you teach me to do that?"

"I'd be delighted when time permits."

Sophy grinned. Raoul was a mesmerizing mentor.

They tiptoed through the shadowy kitchen, lit only by the coals in the range, and up four flights of narrow pine stairs. The nurseries and schoolroom were at the top of the house. The sort of arrangement they had had in the households where Laura had been a governess before she went to the Rannochs'. On her first arrival at the Rannochs' she'd been surprised to find the nursery adjoining Malcolm and Mélanie's bedchamber. Odd to remember that now, with her own and Raoul's bedchamber on the other side of the nursery.

At the top of the stairs, Sophy opened a door onto a narrow passage. The smells of bracing laundry soap, schoolroom chalk, and treacle took Laura back to her days as a governess. And spy.

"I think Miss Tipton will be asleep," Sophy murmured. "Our governess. She'll have put Sally and Billy to bed, but if I know them, they'll be awake." She eased open a door onto a shadowy room lit by the glow of a tin-shaded nightlight. Over Sophy's shoulder Laura glimpsed two empty wrought iron beds. "Ha," Sophy said. "They must be in the day nursery."

She opened the next door down the passage onto shadows and slightly brighter lamplight.

"Soph!" a girl's voice said. "What happened? Did Mama send you home?"

"No. She doesn't know I'm here."

"Did you bring jellies?" a boy's voice asked.

"Not this time. Couldn't. Listen, I need to introduce you to some people." Sophy stepped into the room and gestured for Laura and Raoul to follow. "Mr. and Mrs. O'Roarke."

A girl and boy sat on a blue-and-red hearthrug before the fireplace where banked embers glowed. They had a blanket over their laps, a lamp on the floor beside them, and a box that looked as though it contained caramels. The girl had blonde plaits and a fine-boned face. The boy, who looked to be a couple of years younger, had thick, dark hair spilling over his forehead and a determination in the angle of his jaw that put Laura in mind of Sophy.

Billy and Sally regarded the new arrivals.

"Are you robbers?" Billy asked.

"I think your sister is far too astute to bring robbers into your house," Raoul said.

"Then what are you doing here in the middle of the night? How did you get in?"

"We came up the servants' stairs," Sophy said.

"But you don't have a key."

"Mr. O'Roarke picked the lock."

"See, I said he was a burglar." Billy seemed rather hopeful about the burglar part.

"Perhaps he's a spy," Sally suggested. She looked from Raoul to Laura. "Are you spies?"

"Yes," Laura said.

"Among other things," Raoul said.

"Wizard," Billy said. "Is that why you picked the lock?"

"We picked the lock because we didn't want to rouse the servants," Sophy said.

"So it's an adventure," Sally said. "Is it something to with Marianne?"

Sophy froze, halfway across the nursery. "What makes you say that?"

Sally cast a quick glance at her brother.

"It's all right," Sophy said. "Mr. and Mrs. O'Roarke know something's up with Marianne. That's why we're here. Marianne ran off from the ball. At least she seems to have done."

"Oh, she did," Billy said. "She told us."

Sophy froze, then lunged forwards and dropped down on the hearthrug. "What? She's been here?"

Billy's head swung to the side with almost comical speed as he met his sister's gaze.

Sally's fingers dug into the folds of blanket wadded up in her lap.

Laura moved into the nursery and knelt on the hearthrug facing the children. "It's hard." She looked between the two children, memories of countless nursery exchanges, with her own children and those of others, in her head. "Of course you're loyal to your sister. But she could be in trouble. And we're trying to help her."

"And you should be loyal to me too," Sophy said. "Little beasts," she added under her breath.

"I heard that," Sally said.

"I meant you too." Sophy drew her knees up in a froth of muslin and lace.

Raoul sat beside Laura, moving with his usual soundlessness. "We won't share anything you say," he told the children. "Except to try to help Marianne."

Billy looked at Sally again.

Sally folded her arms across her chest. "All right. Marianne was here. About an hour ago. We were almost asleep. In front of the fire, because we'd made a pact not to go to sleep until they came back from the ball."

"And because we wanted to eat caramels," Billy said.

"That too."

"I woke up when I heard a noise," Billy said. "Fair jumped out of my skin."

"He thought it was a ghost," Sally said.

Billy shot a look at his sister. "Well, she was wearing a pale dress," Billy said. "And her hair's sort of a blondey, ghosty shade."

"She told us not to scream," Sally said. "Well, actually she clapped a hand over Billy's mouth. Billy bit her fingers."

"I didn't mean to. I was scared!"

"And she said she didn't mean to startle us, but she might be gone for a bit and she wanted us to understand."

"I asked if she was going off with Mr. Thornsby," Billy said.

"Why on earth?" Sophy asked.

"Well, she's going to marry him. And people often run away to get married."

"But not to get married to the people they're already engaged to."

"How should I know? It made more sense than anything else I could think of. Anyway, Marianne said no. But she said we weren't to worry, and not to say anything to Mama and Papa. I said, not even to say that we'd seen her? And she said mostly especially not."

"I said that in that case, they were definitely going to worry," Sally said.

"What did your sister say to that?" Raoul asked.

Sally frowned. "She looked worried. Like she hadn't properly thought things through before. But she said we definitely couldn't tell them. That that would make things ten times worse. I asked how we could help—I mean she's our sister, we're supposed to help each other—and she said just by keeping quiet, which was rather deflating."

"I mean, why did she talk to us at all then," Billy said.

"Oh, that's because she came back for the box," Sally said.

"What box?" Billy asked.

"It sits over there." Sally gestured towards a low white-painted shelf under the windows. "At least, it used to. It was a music box that played a bit of Mozart—that naughty song from *Don Giovanni* about the book, although none of the adults would ever actually say as much. Like we haven't all heard it. Like we don't know what it means that he has 1,003 in Spain. Anyway, I used to love to listen to it, but a bit ago Marianne started fussing that I was going to break it. I just left it alone when she was about, and still played it."

Billy sent her an aggrieved look. "You never said."

"I didn't want to kick up a dust and have Marianne take the music box away altogether."

"Didn't you ever look at it to see what she was fussing about so much?"

"Well, yes." Sally squirmed beneath the blanket. "I did look inside it. I think the lining was a bit loose. And I might have seen a corner of paper. But I didn't pull it out. I mean, if Marianne had secrets, they were her secrets. She was so careful in most cases, she deserved whatever secrets she had."

Billy's scowl deepened. "We're supposed to share things."

"We do. Just not Marianne's secrets. You're not good at keeping secrets."

"That's because no one ever tells me any."

"When was it your sister started being particular about the music box?" Raoul asked.

Sally frowned, brows drawn, freckled nose wrinkled. "After the holidays last year—I had my Christmas candy hidden in it and no one noticed. But before my birthday. I remember sneaking the music box out at night as a birthday treat and feeling quite daring because Marianne had lectured me recently. So, before April, I think it was—yes, February. Just after Valentine's Day. She lectured me about getting it sticky with Valentine's chocolates the first time she told me."

"And she had the box tonight?" Laura said.

Billy drew a breath.

"Oh, yes," Sally said without hesitation. "She was holding it under her shawl when she talked to us. She must have picked it up before she woke us. Didn't you see?" she asked Billy.

"No. I might have done, if anyone had admitted it was important."

"There was a bulge under her shawl."

"I wasn't looking at her shawl. I was looking at her face."

"And the music box is gone."

Billy followed his sister's gaze to the shelf. "Yes, I can see that now."

"Did she say anything else?" Laura asked.

"Not really," Sally said.

Billy's face screwed up. "She said she loved us. I suppose that's not really important—"

"On the contrary," Raoul said. "It may be very important indeed."

Sally looked at him. "Because you think it means she may have thought she wouldn't see us again for a while?"

"What do you think?" Raoul said.

Sally's brows tightened. "I think she thought she was saying goodbye." She opened her eyes very wide. In an instant her gaze held the understanding of an adult and the fear of a child.

Laura reached across the hearthrug and gripped Sally's hand. "That's a tremendous help. We'll do everything we can to find your sister."

Raoul reached into his pocket and held out the earring he'd found in the garden. "Do either of you recognize this?"

Billy shook his head, but Sally said, "Oh, yes. I've always liked that pair."

"It was your sister's?" Raoul said.

"No, it's Charlotte's. Charlotte Wilcox."

"Really?" Sophy said. "I didn't recognize it."

"That's because you never pay attention to clothes and jewelry. I've seen her wear them heaps of times. She wore them to Mama's ball for you last month."

"That explains it. I've done everything I could to get the ball out my memory. I suppose Charlotte lost it tonight when she was in the garden with Marianne."

Billy's gaze had settled on Laura. He looked less scared than Sally, but in some ways less reassured. "What if you find Marianne and she doesn't want to come back?"

"Then we'll do everything we can to find out why she doesn't want to come back and try to fix things so she can."

Laura didn't look at Raoul, but she could feel his gaze upon her. Because of course they would try to do that. And of course there was no guarantee they would succeed.

$\mathcal{E}$dith caught Mélanie's arm as Mélanie stepped into the ballroom. "Thank goodness. I've been looking for you everywhere. I actually danced two dances because someone mentioned the young men were friends of Gerry Schofield's, but I didn't learn anything, and I had to avoid being maneuvered under the mistletoe. Have you learned anything?"

"We talked to Miss Wilcox."

"Oh, good. I thought it was best to drop out of the way. That is, I don't know what she knows, but if she knows anything about me at all, it couldn't but be awkward. That is, I don't mean to presume—"

"You aren't presuming at all." Mélanie drew Edith to a settee that had just been vacated by two ladies in plumes and paste diamonds. "You're showing a great deal of sensitivity. I don't know what Miss Wilcox may know about you, but I just spoke with Lucinda Mallinson, who apparently is very good friends with Marianne Schofield and Charlotte Wilcox, and she's well aware of your and Thomas's attachment."

"Did she say Miss Schofield knows?" Edith asked quickly.

"No. She hadn't wanted to speak to Miss Schofield about it."

Edith grabbed her shawl before it could slither off her shoulders. "Lucinda had seen Thomas and me at your house. I doubt Miss Schofield had seen us together. I'd only glimpsed her once or twice. I'm sure Thomas wouldn't have said anything."

"No, but she may have heard gossip."

Edith grimaced. "You don't think that's why she ran off?"

"No. From what Miss Wilcox told us, it's very difficult to tell what made her run off. We have a portrait of a very level-headed and self-contained young woman. Though I also think Miss Wilcox and Lucinda are holding something back."

"You think Miss Schofield was keeping some sort of secret?"

"Nearly everyone has secrets of some sort. I think they know something that may have to do with why Miss Schofield ran. Even tangentially. I also think Miss Schofield was having qualms about her betrothal. She seems to have been following the path her parents wanted."

"A lot of girls do that. You think she regretted it?"

"It seems perhaps she had begun to. It's not clear. Miss Schofield's thoughts seem particularly difficult to read."

Edith spread her hands over the russet sarcenet skirt of her gown. "Is it dreadful that I'm hideously pleased to hear that?"

"I'd be shocked if you weren't," Mélanie said.

"But it's not good for Thomas. He's my friend. I shouldn't want him disappointed."

"Thomas is my friend as well, and I'm trying to be a neutral observer. But it doesn't appear to me that he's particularly happy in his betrothal."

For a moment something shot through Edith's gaze. Then she glanced away, the fire banked. "He still needs to marry a fortune. And it's not as though I—marriage is complicated."

"So it is."

Edith's gaze shot to Mélanie's face. Do you ever wish you'd made a different choice?"

"Constantly. Which choice in particular are you wondering about?" Mélanie said.

"Getting married." Edith colored. "Oh, I know that sounds absurd. You have such a splendid marriage and Malcolm is so understanding. But it must—I mean, there are things you have to do as a wife. I don't mean *those* things." Her color deepened. "I mean, that's one of the appealing things about marriage, it seems to me. At least, with the right person. And the right person would never insist— But I mean—you can't simply do as you want anymore. Not all the time."

"No," Mélanie agreed. "That's true." She checked the easy denial, partly because that wasn't what Edith wanted and partly because it wouldn't be true. She jumped to her feet, snatched two glasses of champagne from a passing footman, and gave one to Edith. "Everyone gives up things in a marriage. You have to think about someone else when you make choices. Sometimes several other people, if you have children."

"But women have to give up more than men."

Malcolm would never ask me to give up anything. That was the obvious answer. And yet she had been giving things up from the start. Her very name and identity, though that had only been because she was a spy. Later she'd given up her work as a spy to stay married to him. She'd pretended to a background and beliefs and loyalties that weren't her own. She took a drink of champagne. Yeasty and smooth, but it had a bite. "Often."

"But you don't think you have?"

"At the start, perhaps." Well, after she stopped spying on him. No, while she was spying on him. Because there was no denying she'd suppressed a lot of herself. Mélanie took another drink of champagne, conflicting feelings tumbling through her. The orchestra had moved into a waltz. One that had been popular in Paris after Waterloo, when she'd first stopped spying and had been dancing and dining with the victors while her former comrades faced prison and execution. "I thought I had to be a sort of perfect diplomatic wife. And then a political wife. He never asked it of me. But it was—"

"What society expected."

"And what I thought I owed him." All the more because of the reasons they'd married. "We were both solitary people. But I suppose I dove more into the business of trying to make a home. I'd never seen myself as domestic, but one of us had to pull our household together." And there'd been so much else she couldn't do, especially when she stopped spying. "He'd often forget to tell me if he'd be home to dinner." Even later, in London, so much of her life had revolved round entertaining and accepting invitations. In some ways she'd been the most herself when she helped with his speeches. But they were still *his* speeches. "But things started to change after we went to Italy. We both realized we had different priorities. I started writing plays."

Edith twisted the stem of her glass between her fingers. "But if you weren't married you could write more."

Mélanie checked the instinctive denial. But of course that was true. Even if she had no family obligations, she'd undoubtedly reach a point where the words would blur on the page and she couldn't write any more without a break, but she would have more time without a family to claim her attention. "Well, yes. I'd have more time if I didn't investigate mysteries as well. And if I wasn't a mother. That doesn't mean I wish I wasn't any of those things."

"So you don't ever wonder?" Edith's face was intent, the look of a scholar trying to puzzle out an elusive truth. "What it would be like if you weren't married?"

A world she'd never really let herself imagine hovered just beyond her consciousness. "Mostly I'm aware of how much I'd miss that I have now."

"I mean—you can't simply get up when you want and take your coffee from a coffee stall and then come home and bury yourself in your work. I suppose that sounds petty—"

"No, it sounds quite delightful in many ways. But then, so does waking up to the children bounding into our bedchamber and pouncing on the bed, and drinking coffee while playing hide-and-seek, and writing while they play and while Malcom works on one of his speeches and we trade pages back and forth." Mélanie twisted the diamond and white-gold chain bracelet Malcolm had given her round her wrist. Edith deserved honest answers. Edith was different from her, of course. Everyone had to figure out what happiness meant to them. But it seemed vitally important she answer as honestly as she could. And honesty was always hard for a spy.

"But do you ever wonder who you'd be if you'd made a different choice?" Edith asked. "Do you ever think—not that you'd be happier if you'd made a different choice, but that you'd be more yourself? Able to live life on your own terms?"

I feel more myself when I'm with Malcolm than any other time. That was the obvious answer. And when it first dawned on her that she loved him she'd thought that he knew her as no one else ever had. At least so she had felt in that moment. But at other times, she had felt so lost in her masquerade spying on her husband that she wasn't sure who she was anymore, beneath the façade of Mrs. Malcolm Rannoch. And then, after she'd stopped spying, she'd felt in many ways that she'd lost the core of herself. The core that was Mélanie, not a wife, not a mother, not a political and diplomatic hostess. She thought about the times she brought Malcolm coffee, helped tidy his papers, made his life easier in ways he wasn't even aware of. He'd never asked for any of it. He probably wasn't even aware of the time she took to do it. Part of her had felt she owed it to him because of everything she'd done to him. Which was a fair point. And there was no denying he did a great deal for her. And yet—

"If I hadn't married Malcolm, I'd be a different person. I can't say I'd be more or less myself, because marrying Malcolm changed me. In ways I wouldn't give up for anything. Being Colin and Jessica's mother constantly changes me. I can't imagine another life. But I can see how someone else might make different choices. And still be happy. I can't say you wouldn't give up anything if you married. Though I can say with certainty I'd be lonelier if I hadn't."

Edith took a drink of champagne. "I like solitude. Not all the time, but sometimes. I don't know that I'm very good at fussing over people. I'm not sure I'd make Thomas at all happy. That is, even if we could—and we can't, so it's silly to think about it."

"I don't know that one can stop thinking about it. And I think it's rather up to Thomas to decide what would make him happy in a wife. Because, while I do perhaps fuss over Malcolm more than he realizes, overall he doesn't want it and would loathe it if I did more."

"Thomas is stubborn, but someone else would make him happier."

"Oh, I used to be convinced a number of women would have made Malcolm happier. Often it was just a vague sense that there'd have been a perfect wife for him who'd know everything I didn't and fit seamlessly into his world. But then, there was one woman in particular whom I think he came closer to marrying than he'd ever admit, who I was quite sure would have done so."

"Do you still think so?" Edith asked.

Mélanie drew a breath and pictured Honoria Talbot's shining golden hair. "Oddly enough, no. We saw her in the investigation in October. And that changed things." In ways she hadn't realized until now.

"So you never wonder if he'd be happier?"

Constantly. Every day. But marrying your husband to spy on him rather changed the equation of how one viewed one's husband in the aftermath. "Malcolm's a different person as well." Less withdrawn. Happier, perhaps. And also less inclined to trust, for which she would never quite forgive herself. "I don't think I could not but wonder sometimes. Doesn't one question everything in one's life at times? But I'm quite sure he'd say he's happier as well."

Edith set her champagne glass on the table beside the settee and rubbed her arms, creasing her gloves. "I don't think I'm suited to it."

"I didn't think I was either. For that matter, I'm not sure I am. If I weren't married to Malcolm, I don't think I'd want to be married. But I am glad I'm married to Malcolm."

Edith looked away. "I'm quite sure I'd make a mull of it. So you'd think I'd be happy Thomas is betrothed and out of reach." She stared down at her rumpled gloves. "Damn."

"One can debate the connection between love and marriage," Mélanie said. "But there's no denying love can be tenacious."

Edith snatched up her glass and tossed down the last of the champagne. "Even when it's hopeless."

CHAPTER 14

$\mathcal{A}$ young woman in a spangled peach dress came careering up the stairs and nearly hurtled into Julien and Kitty. Julien put a steadying hand on her gloved arm. "Are you all right, miss?"

"Oh, I'm so sorry."

Julien released the young woman, assured she was secure on her feet. She had nut-brown hair slipping from its pins, and clear brown eyes. "It's difficult in such a crowd. May my wife and I help you find your way back to your family?"

"Oh, no, I'm not—That is, I can manage on my own."

Julien smiled. For a hardened agent, he had always, Kitty thought, had surprisingly kind smiles. "You appeared intent on getting somewhere. May we help you find someone?"

The girl drew a quick breath.

"My apologies," Julien said. "There is no one here to introduce us. My name is Julien. Julien Mallinson, if I must add more."

Her eyes widened. "You're Lord Carfax."

"Unfortunately. My wife Kitty."

"I'm Justine. Justine Lambton."

"Are you looking for someone, Miss Lambton?" Kitty asked.

"No. Yes. But—Do you know Gerry—Gerald Schofield?"

"Gerry Schofield?" Harry materialized out of the crowd beside them.

"Miss Lambton," Julien said by way of introduction. "Harry Davenport."

Justine Lambton's eyes lit up. "The classicist? You wrote *The Many Faces of Livia?*"

Genuine surprise crossed Harry's face. For someone so brilliant, he was, Kitty thought, distinctly unassuming about his work. "I am. You follow classical studies?"

"Oh yes. I always have. My father tutors classics."

"So you've grown up in the world of classical studies."

"Sort of. Mostly seeing undergraduates come for tutoring sessions and my father shake his head."

"And I imagine you know a great deal more than most of those undergraduates yourself."

"Well, yes. That is, often. Quite disagreeable. I should love to go a meeting of the Classicists' Society."

"There's no reason you shouldn't. But—forgive me, you said you were looking for Gerry Schofield? Would your given name happen to be Justine?"

"How can you—I've heard you were an intelligence agent, but—"

"It's less any sort of investigative ability than the fact that I happen to have just been speaking with Mr. Schofield," Harry said. "He mentioned you. Or at least he mentioned a quite brilliant scholar named Justine, whose father is a Cambridge tutor."

Justine flushed, then started. "Gerry's here? Thank goodness. You've seen him?"

"I was just speaking with him. And it sounds as though you need to see him as soon as possible?"

"Yes, please!"

EDITH GAVE a polite smile to the young man she had just stumbled through the Boulanger with. Whitcombe or Whitfield or something of the sort. Thank goodness he was promised to the someone else for the next dance. She stepped off the dance floor and found herself looking straight at Thomas Thornsby.

Well in fairness they were several feet apart, but their gazes locked, and it seemed more awkward than to turn away than to walk forwards.

"I'm afraid I haven't learned anything, " she said.

"Nor have I. But I think the others may be faring better. "

"I wish I could help more. "

"Edith. It was kind of you to come at all." His voice caught. The air suddenly felt thick between them.

The crowd eddied all round them, voices rose and fell, the orchestra was moving into a new dance, but this was the closest they had come to being alone since Thomas's betrothal.

"I owe you an apology," Thomas said in a low voice.

"You don't owe me anything at all, Thomas. We'd made no promises to each other. We always knew where we stood."

"I'm not very proud of myself."

"You're making a sacrifice for the good of your family. That is —" Edith drew a breath that made her think of Portia swallowing coals. "I'm making a rather presumptuous presumption."

"No," Thomas said quickly. "You must know—you can't doubt that this isn't what I'd have chosen. It seemed as though it could work. As though at least I wasn't offering Marianne false coin. Now I doubt even that."

"I'm not sure what I think of marriage, but people have all sorts of reasons for doing it. Perhaps Miss Schofield was—is— getting what she wants out of it."

"So I told myself. That seems less likely now she's disappeared."

The new dance was a waltz. She and Thomas has danced to it once. Damn, she wasn't going to give way to sentiment. "I won't pretend to be happy about the situation, Thomas. But there's no shame in marrying to oblige your family. Quite the opposite. You know I was never sure we were suited."

"And Marianne and I am?"

"That's rather for you and Miss Schoflied to sort out. And I suppose it depends on the sort of life you want."

"That *I* want? You have to know—"

"We'd have had a very untidy life, Thomas. I'm not a tidy person."

His mouth twisted in a faint smile. "I could use some more untidiness in my life. I—" He bit back whatever he'd been going to say. "Right now all I know is that I need to find Marianne. I'll never forgive myself if some harm has befallen her because of me."

"I'm here to help."

"I can't ask you—"

"Rubbish. I'd be a poor creature if I stood by while someone was in trouble. If she's going to be your wife, she's the wife of one of my best friends. And even if not, she's your friend."

"You're—amazing, Edith."

"Don't talk rot, Thomas, we haven't time for it."

MÉLANIE SPOTTED Raoul on the edge of the ballroom. One would swear he had been strolling about all evening, but she knew (because they had sent word to her before they left) that he and Laura must have just returned with Sophy Schofield. Though there was no sign of Laura or Sophy.

Mélanie slipped to his side through the throng. "Did you learn anything?"

"Marianne Schofield returned home this evening and saw her younger brother and sister." Raoul took two glasses of champagne from a passing footman and handed her one as though they were engaged in casual conversation. "From what she said to them, it sounded as though she thought she'd be gone for some time. And she retrieved a music box in which it sounds as though she had hidden letters."

"Love letters?"

"That's an obvious assumption. But I think it's possible it's something to do with her father." Raoul lifted his glass to his lips, barely touching the champagne but giving a perfect impression of a gentleman indulging in light flirtation with a lady at a ball. "I have a bit of history with Miss Schofield's father." Smiling as though they were exchanging banter, Raoul described his association with Marianne Schofield's father.

Mélanie stared at him, sipping from her own glass and trying to match his insouciance. "And we thought we'd escaped espionage."

"We never will, *querida*. But I confess this surprised me. And given our history, it's all too easy to jump to certain conclusions. We should alert the others."

Mélanie glanced round the ballroom. "Where are Laura and Sophia Schofield?"

"We came in through the garden. They went into the house. I climbed the stairs to the balcony. Always better not to have the whole team move together."

"You'll never stop thinking like a spymaster."

"I hope not. I also hope I'm not overthinking." Raoul glanced round the ballroom. "We should find them and the others."

"Raoul?" Mélanie asked as they threaded their way across the room.

She said it softly, almost too much so to hear, but he paused and looked back at her over his shoulder. Again, the entire gesture and expression could have passed for a casual interchange. Save for the look in his eyes. "What is it, *querida?*"

Mélanie hesitated. She talked to Raoul more easily than anyone except probably Malcolm. Or Cordy, on occasion. And yet — "Edith asked me if I ever wondered what my life would have been like if I hadn't married."

Raoul took a few steps forwards, then turned back to her, one hand resting on a gilded column garlanded with pine. "What did you say?"

"That mostly I was incredibly grateful I wasn't the person I'd have been alone. But then she asked me if I thought I'd have been more myself on my own. And I couldn't—"

"Couldn't what?" His gaze stayed steady on her face.

"Don't be provoking, you know what I mean." She unfurled her fan for the benefit of anyone watching. "I'd be a different person if I hadn't married Malcolm. I wouldn't be anywhere near the beau monde. Well, not unless I was on a mission."

"Which is mostly why you go out in the beau monde these days. Such as tonight."

"Well, yes, but I wouldn't have built a life there. Here. I wouldn't have had vouchers to Almack's or a house in Berkeley Square or a box at the Tavistock."

"You'd be backstage as a playwright. Or acting onstage."

"Precisely. It's not—it's one thing for Malcolm, it's the life he was born to. But for me it goes against everything I claim to believe in."

Raoul held out his arm to her. "If it comes to that, it goes against everything I believe in to be living at the heart of the aristocracy."

Mélanie curled her fingers round his arm. "You were born in the aristocracy." Far more than she'd realized when she first met him.

He gave a faint smile. "A palpable hit. But I wouldn't have lived in—"

"You were living in it when you met Arabella Rannoch. Or you wouldn't have met her. You've moved in it your whole life, even if you were spying."

"Fair enough. But I wouldn't be living here, in Berkeley Square, and moving in some of the circles I do now." His gaze went across the room where Emily Cowper stood with her lover, Lord

Palmerston, who had both been instrumental in their most recent investigation. "I doubt I'd be laughing with Lord Palmerston and Emily Cowper as old friends. Not if it weren't for Arabella and Malcolm and Laura. And you. We all shape our lives to the people we care about. That doesn't make us any less ourselves. It may make us more so." He watched her for a moment and she could tell he was reading the emotions flitting across her face, and seeing more in them than she ever would have been able to put into words, even to herself. "You must know I never thought to, never intended to, have another child. One could fairly argue that I'm not the most responsible father. But if I hadn't become a father again, I'd be living my life differently. For that matter, if Malcolm hadn't been born, I'd have lived my life differently. And I'd be immeasurably poorer for it."

"But would you be—"

"More myself? Who's to say what that means? I far prefer the person I am now."

"But do you ever wonder—"

His mouth twisted. "I told Laura once that I questioned the choices I'd made every day of my life. That was true then. I question my recent choices far less. Do I sometimes wonder if I could be a better father and husband? Frequently. Do I sometimes wonder if I could be doing more in Spain? At times. Would I change any of the things I have now? No. I'm astonished by my good fortune every day." He watched her for a long moment. The light from the candle sconce above shifted between them. "I didn't expect to be a father at twenty to a child I couldn't publicly claim. I didn't expect the Elsinore League. And if I expected a revolution, it wasn't the one we got. But I've been able to define my own life far more than you have. There are a number of choices you never got to make."

"I've made choices. I take full responsibility for them."

"Granted. But your options were limited. I think you may have just found your way back to what you might have chosen."

"The theatre?"

"And a way to use your voice. But having a family doesn't mean the end of being able to make choices."

"I tried to tell Edith that. Though I'm not sure it's for everyone. She has to decide if it's for her. It's easy to see it as a sort of obvious happy ending. In fiction. And in life." Mélanie drew a breath. "For years I wasn't sure if I knew who the real me was. To be honest, for a while I wasn't sure if there *was* a real me anymore. That's begun to change."

"I'm glad. Talking of things I question."

"You gave me a chance to be myself. If I hadn't become an agent, I'm not sure what would have happened to me."

Raoul's expression stilled. "You saved yourself."

She gathered up the folds of her gown as they slipped between two young couples laughing over champagne and a trio of ladies intent on gossip. "I used to think domesticity was a trap," she said.

"I used to think it was beyond me. That in the life I lived I could never risk it."

"So you did think it would change you?"

"I thought I couldn't change enough to make it work. In the end, I did change. But not as much as I might have thought I'd have to. Perhaps not as much as I should have done."

"Oh, well," Mélanie said. "I frequently feel as though I'm failing on three or four fronts at once. But that's being a—"

"An agent?"

She tightened her fingers on his arm and took a step forwards. "A parent."

CHAPTER 15

"Justine!" A young man who Kitty assumed was Gerry Schofield went skidding across the floorboards of the sitting room where Justine was waiting with Kitty and Julien. "What are you doing here?"

"Gerry, thank goodness." Justine sprang to her feet.

Kitty, who had been sitting next to Justine, got to her feet as well. "We'll let you talk alone." She met Julien's gaze. One could not but be curious, but there was no reason to think this had anything to do with Marianne Schofield's disappearance.

"No, please," Justine said. "That is, I've heard you investigate things. I think that might be precisely what we need." She looked at Gerry. "Do you know Lord and Lady Carfax?"

"Not precisely," Gerry said. "But I know they work with the Rannochs and Davenports. Oh, we haven't been introduced—"

"I don't think we need to waste time on formalities," Julien said. "We seem to be in the midst of multiple crises."

"Davenport's already in the midst of this," Gerry said. He looked at Harry, who moved away from the door, then looked back at Justine. "Davenport knows. About your articles and the Forum." He looked at Julien and Kitty as though suddenly realizing they didn't know. "Justine's a classicist. She writes quite brilliantly—"

"And you published her articles in the Forum under a different name?" Julien said.

Gerry and Justine both stared at him. "How on earth did you know that?" Gerry asked.

"You'll get used to it," Kitty said. "It looks like witchcraft but it's really just piecing together information."

"I had to tell Davenport," Gerry said. "That is, I had to explain about why I was sent down, because they were assuming all sorts of wrong things. About that and about Marianne."

"What about your sister?" Justine asked.

"Oh. Marianne's missing."

"Missing?"

"Yes, she disappeared from the ball. It's complicated. I think. But I daresay it's nothing to do with this. With why you're here. That is—"

"It's Papa," Justine said. "I know you wanted to keep it quiet about the Forum and everything, and I agreed to protect him, but now everyone knows."

"Everyone?" Gerry said.

"Well, someone does. We had a letter delivered to the house."

"A letter about the papers?"

Justine's shoulders tightened. "Papa wouldn't show it to me at first. In fact, he crumpled it up and tossed it on the fire. I had to retrieve it with the tongs after he left the room and part of it was burnt. But it said, 'We know who wrote the papers in the Forum. Don't deny it.'"

Gerry jerked and seized Justine's hands again. "What did you do then?"

"I went to Papa and said we had to talk. He said there was nothing to talk about. Obviously, we weren't going to do anything. I said, but I wrote those papers. And he just looked at me. You know the way Papa can look at one. And said"—Justine drew a breath, fluttering the sleeves of her gown—"'My dear child, of course you did. I knew that the moment I saw them. I can recognize your style, and I could hardly fail to be a proud parent when I read what you had written.'"

"What an excellent parent," Harry said.

Justine shot a quick smile at him. "It was rather splendid, I confess. Except that it doesn't change the fact that he could get into trouble. I said as much and he said to let him worry about that, which of course was stuff. I mean, I'm not a baby anymore." She glanced at Harry again, and then at Julien and Kitty. "Can you understand?"

"As the father of two daughters, I can understand both your father's desire to protect you and your determination to look after yourself," Harry said.

"Quite," Kitty said. "One does want to spare one's children."

"Yes, but I'm quite grown up now."

"Forgive me," Julien said, "but I think to a parent, one's children are never entirely grown up."

"Well, yes. I supposed I can sort of see that."

Gerry tightened his grip on Justine's hands. "What happened then?"

"Then?"

"Yes, after your father told you not to worry about it. How did you convince him to come to London?"

"Oh, Papa's not in London. That would have made a mull of everything."

Gerry stared at her. "Then what are you doing here?"

"Well, naturally, I couldn't leave it at that. I knew I had to talk to you. So I went to Arthur Dashwood. I knew he was coming to town for his sister's wedding. I begged him to take me with him. At first he said he couldn't. But when I said I was going to go on the stage, he finally agreed. So he gave me a seat in the carriage his parents sent. He kept fussing about how I didn't have a chaperone, but I said I wasn't going to talk and I trusted he wouldn't." She cast a quick look from Harry to Julien and Kitty to Gerry.

"Absolutely not," Harry said.

"Word of honor," Julien said. Quite seriously, though he never talked seriously about honor.

"We wouldn't dream of it," Kitty said.

"Oh yes. Of course," Gerry said.

"Well, then. It was silly to worry. When we got to London, he took me to Gerry's house and went up to the door with me, but when the footman said none of the family were at home, Gerry said he knew Lady Cowper was giving a ball tonight, and he thought he could get in because his mother and sisters were going. So he brought me here. Though first we sneaked into his house and he gave me one of his sister's dresses." She smoothed the skirt of her gold-spangled peach gauze. It set off her hair and eyes, but the peach satin sash gathered up a skirt that was meant for someone with a larger frame.

"It's pretty," Gerry said.

"It doesn't really fit properly. But I thought it would keep people from staring."

"I'm not sure about that. That is, I think they may stare, for different reasons."

Justine blushed and shook her head. "Don't be silly, Gerry. But you see why I needed to find you."

"Of course. We can't let your father come to grief over this. I can admit the whole."

"Hardly the wisest course," Julien said, "as that would put Justine and her father conclusively in the middle of it."

"Oh, yes. Of course." Gerry dug a hand into his hair. "Just what we were trying to avoid. But there must be some way—"

"Who do you think wrote the letter?" Kitty asked.

Justine frowned. "I didn't recognize the hand. It was dark. Strong writing, if you know what I mean. Good ink—the kind that doesn't streak."

"The paper?"

"Heavy cream laid. Hot-pressed. More a notecard than a full sheet of paper. The sort that might have someone's name embossed, but not all the paper was there."

"You have the instincts of an investigator," Harry said.

"It's part of research, isn't it? Noting details. I expect that's what makes you a good agent."

"Yes. To the extent I have any talent for it, I suspect you're right." Harry moved into the room. "Who might have known enough of the truth to threaten your father? To go to your father, they must have known more than just that the name of the author was made up."

"Yes, I do see that." Justine looked at Gerry.

"I didn't tell anyone," Gerry said. "I wouldn't. Even Dashwood doesn't know all of it."

"He suspects," Justine said.

"Well, yes, I suppose he must. But he wouldn't tell anyone."

"You have a distinctive style," Harry said to Justine. "Someone who had seen your work might have recognized it in the Forum. Whom else had you shared it with?"

"Papa and Gerry. Not many others. I mean, it wasn't exactly a secret, but people don't ask. It meant a lot when Gerry did."

"Are there people who would want to hurt your father?" Kitty asked.

"Papa?" Justine gave a laugh that choked in her throat. "He's the sweetest man imaginable. His students love him, even the hopeless ones. Perhaps especially the hopeless ones, because he helps them, though the clever ones love learning from him and debating ideas with him. He doesn't have an enemy in the world."

"Like my sister," Gerry said.

"Oh, Gerry." Justine gripped his hands, seemingly heedless of Kitty, Julien, and Harry. "I'm so sorry. I should have said that sooner. Do you know what happened?"

"No. It's why I told Davenport and the others about us—you.

The papers and the Forum. Not that I can see how it could have anything to do with Marianne, but they thought it might."

Justine scanned his face. "How? What could I have to do with your sister's disappearing?"

"Not you, but they thought you might have come to see Marianne. That is, they thought a woman I might have—er—known at Cambridge might have come to see her. Someone who might have had something to do with—er—why I was sent down. So I had to explain it wasn't anything like that at all. The reason I was sent down. So they wouldn't waste time. Probably should have been able to come up with a better story."

"No, of course not." Justine's voice was crisp, though she couldn't quite meet Gerry's gaze. "I quite understand. I'm glad you told them." She glanced from Kitty to Julien to Harry, and seemed better able to meet their gazes. "You don't think the articles in the Forum and the letter to Papa have anything to do with Gerry's sister disappearing?"

"I'm not sure," Harry said. "We don't know why Miss Schofield left this evening. But it's possible she received some sort of threatening communication. And your father did as well."

"Yes, but Justine's father doesn't have anything to do with Marianne," Gerry said. "I mean, the only connection is—me."

"An interesting point," Julien said.

"Yes, but—you can't think someone is sending threatening letters to people I care about. Why? I'm completely unimportant."

"No one's unimportant. But motive usually comes down to gain. Or to what someone sees as gain. The question would be what would someone feel they had to gain from threatening Miss Lambton's father and your sister. Your father and Justine's father were friends, you said?"

"Well, yes. When they were at Cambridge."

"We move in quite different circles now," Justine said.

"Not that," Gerry said quickly. "But Papa went to London after university and started his business, and then he married Mama—"

"And they have a grand London life," Justine said.

"Not so very grand. But Papa can hardly conjugate a Latin verb now. I wondered how he ever managed to finish his degree."

"Had Marianne ever met Miss Lambton's father?" Kitty asked.

"Not since we were small. Well, once more recently. Marianne came to visit me at Cambridge with Papa. Justine and her father had them in for tea. So Justine met Marianne too." Gerry cast a quick look at Justine.

"Yes, we did talk in the garden for a bit," Justine said. "While Papa was showing your father his study. I quite liked your sister. Though she seemed—"

"What?" Gerry scanned Justine's face. "Did she say anything disagreeable to you?"

"Oh no. She's very kind. Just like you. And not in the least great lady-ish. I had quite a different image of what a girl would be like who was in the midst of a London season. In fact, she seemed quite interested in my research and the fact that I wrote. She said it must be nice to have something one cared for so much. That was what struck me. That she seemed—" Justine hesitated, fingering the folds of her borrowed gown.

"What?" Gerry asked.

"Not happy." Justine met his gaze. "I don't mean she seemed miserable, and perhaps I misread the situation entirely—"

"No." Gerry regarded her. "That's—I agree with you. That is, I wouldn't have put it that way, but . . ." He broke off, frowning. "I always thought Marianne wanted to be a success in society and find a husband and get married, because that's what girls want."

"I don't," Justine said.

"Yes, but you're—"

"Not a girl?"

"No, I know perfectly well that you are. That is—you're different. You have classics." Gerry looked at Harry. "Lady Cordelia's a classicist."

"Yes, now. She always has been, in a sense. But she'd be the first to say she had other interests during her season."

"The thing is, Marianne doesn't have interests at all." Gerry dug a hand into his hair. "Or maybe she does, and I just don't realize. I told Davenport—I was happy at first that she got engaged to Thornsby. But even then, it kept tugging at the back of my mind that they didn't look like an engaged couple were supposed to look. Not that I know. But I wouldn't—"

"Want to look like that with your betrothed?" Julien said.

"Yes. No. I mean, I have no thought of getting betrothed. But if I did—no, that isn't how I'd want it to be." Gerry shifted his weight from one foot to another.

"She said it was hard," Justine said.

"What was hard?"

"Knowing what to go after in life. She said she envied my knowing that. I thought it was so odd, her envying me." Justine wrinkled her nose. "And yet, I must say I prefer my life. That is—"

"No," Gerry said. "I understand."

Justine met his gaze in a moment of understanding. "She said she'd thought once she had her season it would all make sense. That she was working for something and then she'd understand it. But she said the closer she got the less it made sense."

"What made sense?" Gerry asked.

"She didn't say precisely. But I sort of thought she meant marrying and the whole bit. Like it was a sort of goal she'd been reaching for, and now it was in reach she wasn't sure she wanted it."

"You mean like a Praetorian guard who was scheming to become emperor and then had doubts as his coup was about to succeed?" Gerry asked.

Justine choked. "Not precisely. Your sister didn't strike me as a schemer at all. More like someone who was brought up to be emperor as the heir to the throne and never questioned it, and then suddenly started questioning if they wanted the life they'd been bred for. But no other choice seemed possible."

"Are you saying you think my sister ran away because she didn't want to marry Thornsby?"

"I can't say what your sister did, Gerry. I only met her once."

"But would you? Run away because you didn't want to marry a man?"

"Yes. Well, no. I'd never agree to marry a man I didn't want to marry. I can't imagine getting married at all, but I certainly wouldn't agree to it unless I really wanted to."

"So you'd run away?"

"I'd probably just break the engagement. Or not accept the gentleman in the first place. But perhaps Marianne was afraid of causing a scandal."

"What on earth does she think we're all so worried about now from her disappearing?" Gerry said. "That's a crackbrained notion. And Marianne's always been the sensible one in the family."

"Everyone has moments when they lack sense," Kitty said.

"Or she could have eloped," Justine said.

Gerry stared at her.

"I mean, it's an obvious reason someone would run off when they're supposed to marry someone else," Justine said.

"Yes, but with who? Whom? It's not that there's someone she wanted instead of Thornsby. I mean, not from anything we could tell."

"Well, presumably, if she eloped it would be with someone she thought everyone thought was unsuitable."

"You mean a penniless curate or something?"

"Or a footman."

"Good God."

"People don't just fall in love with people from their own circles," Julien pointed out.

"No. I understand that. But—"

"We don't know that that's what happened with your sister,"

Justine said. "We're just trying to figure out why she may have disappeared."

The door burst open. Sophy Schofield came running into the room, Laura close behind her. "Marianne went home," Sophy announced, the words tumbling fast as her satin-slippered feet thudded across the floor. "She gathered up the music box from the nursery. Sally says there were some papers hidden in it. And from what Marianne said to Sally and Billy, they think she thought she'd be gone for a while."

"What did she say?" Gerry took a step towards his sister.

"Just that she was going. We don't know where. If—" Sophy cast a glance round the room and froze when she caught sight of Justine, standing just behind Gerry. "Who are you?"

CHAPTER 16

Gerry Schofield looked from his sister to Justine. "Oh, this is Just—Miss Lambton. My sister Sophy."

Sophy's gaze moved over Justine. "You're the girl Gerry's barmy about."

"What?" Gerry said as Justine blushed. "No! That is—"

"My father is your brother's tutor," Justine said.

"Yes, I know," Sophy said. "Your father and ours went to Cambridge together. I think we met when we were very small. Papa says your father was the most loyal friend he ever had. And Gerry's always talking about him. Though more about you."

"Soph!" The look Gerry gave his sister would probably have been combined with a kick in the ankle had he been situated to do so. "Justine needed to see me about something. She knows about Marianne. Never mind how, for now. Why did Billy and Sally say Marianne left?"

"They didn't. They don't know. You know Marianne, she never tells anyone anything. Mr. and Mrs. O'Roarke were splendid at asking questions." Sophy turned to gesture to Laura. In the process, her gaze fell on Harry. "Who are you?"

"Colonel Davenport," Gerry said. "He's a friend. And a classi-cist. And a spy. And these are Lord and Lady Carfax."

"Oh, yes, we met ages ago. Well, I suppose it wasn't much more than an hour, but it seems like ages ago. They prefer to be called Julien and Kitty. If—"

A rap sounded at the door. Stillness gripped the room. Julien moved to the door with languid ease and opened it, his body angled to prevent anyone outside from entering should it prove necessary. Over her husband's shoulder, Kitty could see a footman outside the door. Not one of the footmen she recalled seeing before at Emily Cowper's, though she hadn't been a guest in the house often enough to say she knew all of them. But she suspected this man had been hired for the night.

"Forgive me," the footman said. "Is Mr. Schofield here?"

"Yes." Gerry took a step forwards. "What is it?"

Julien moved aside. The footman stepped into the room and held a sealed paper out. "I was asked to give this to you. It's for a Miss Lambton. I was told you'd know where to find her."

Gerry stared but had the presence of mind not to glance at Justine. "Thank you."

The footman withdrew. Gerry held the note out to Justine.

Justine stared down at it. "But who even knows I'm in London, let alone at this ball?"

"Do you recognize the hand?" Harry asked.

She shook her head and slit the seal, stared at the note for a moment with puzzled eyes, then held it out for all of them to look at.

If you value your father's safety, come to No. 43 Conduit Street.
Don't let anyone see you leave the ball.

"What on earth?" Gerry said. "Who could be threatening your father?"

"I don't know. But I have to go."

"Yes." Harry said. "You do."

"What?" Gerry stared at him. "It's too dangerous."

"I wasn't suggesting she go alone. But we need to learn who is behind this."

"I was thinking that," Justine said. "It has to look as though I'm alone, but if you could follow me that would be much better." She looked from Harry to Kitty to Julien. "I'm not an idiot. It's idiotic to go rushing off into danger on one's own. Perhaps you'll have an idea of how to follow me without being seen, Colonel Davenport? I haven't the least idea, but it seems the sort of thing an agent can arrange."

"It can be arranged," Julien said.

"I'm helping," Gerry said.

Julien smiled at him. "I assumed as much."

"I'm coming too," Sophy said.

"Naturally," Julien said.

"You mean you'll let us?" Sophy asked. "Even though we're civilians?"

"We count on your doing as told," Julien said.

"So we're sensible enough to stay out of the way?" Sophy asked.

"Often that's half the trick of a successful mission," Kitty said. "The best agents are expert at staying out of the way. Ask my husband. He almost never gets in my way."

"I do my best," Julien said.

RAOUL WENT STILL, his gaze fixed across the ballroom. "This is interesting."

Amid the swirling crowd, his gaze had fastened on a tall man of middle years, with sandy blond hair and slightly stooped shoulders. The man caught Raoul's gaze and went still. Raoul strode forwards, without obvious haste but too quickly for the gentleman to escape.

"Schofield," Raoul said in an easy voice. "It's been a long time."

Theodore Schofield's pale complexion had turned as green as the stripes on his silk waistcoat. "O'Roarke. A pleasant surprise."

"I move in society a bit more than I used to." Raoul's easy voice gave no hint that his prior dealings with Schofield had almost certainly been confined to espionage, yet his gaze did not allow Schofield to move. "Lady Cowper is close to our friends the Rannochs." He turned to Mélanie. "You know Mrs. Rannoch?"

Theodore Schofield inclined his head.

"Mr. Schofield." Mélanie returned the nod. She had shaken hands with him once or twice at large events. "I understand I am to felicitate you on your daughter's betrothal."

"Yes, thank you." Schofield put up a hand to his neckcloth. "Thornsby is an admirable young man." He turned to Raoul. "I haven't had the chance to congratulate you on your own marriage."

"Thank you." Raoul's voice continued friendly, but something about his easy stance had never looked more like a panther. "I am beyond fortunate. I never thought to find myself a husband and father of young children at this age. But I think a number of us have found our lives have changed in different ways since Waterloo."

"Indeed." Thornsby took a gulp from his glass of champagne. "I have been fortunate myself."

A footman approached them and turned to Schofield. "Mr. Schofield? I have a letter for you."

He held out a sealed paper. Schofield's green complexion drained to parchment white. He slit the seal, stared at the paper, and then turned his gaze to Raoul and Mélanie. Mélanie, prepared for him to make his excuses, was wondering how they could follow him. But Schofield said simply, "I need your help."

"Anything?" Edith stopped beside Malcolm on the edge of the dance floor. "I'm sorry that sounds horrid. I just can't bear not being able to do anything."

"I know the feeling." Malcolm touched her arm. "Emily just told me one of the footmen thinks he saw a young woman go out the garden gate. But that just confirms what we suspected. Nothing else definitive. That I know of. A lot of us are working on this at once."

Cordelia joined them. "I must have talked to a dozen people, all of whom had glimpsed Marianne Schofield at some point and none of whom could remember when. The only good thing I can report is that I think I managed it all without betraying that my interest in Marianne had to do with anything but gossip about the latest betrothed couple."

"Everyone goes silent about anything to do with Marianne and Thomas whenever I so much as walk by," Edith said. "So I'm quite hopeless in this investigation. But I do think Marianne's disappearance hasn't been noticed yet."

"So do I," Malcolm said. "Which would be comforting if we were any closer to discovering the truth. I hope Raoul and Laura learned something, but I haven't seen them."

Cordelia frowned. "I haven't seen Harry for some time. Perhaps—"

"Malcolm." Thomas Thornsby materialized out of the crowd beside them, then went still at the sight of Edith.

"I'll leave," Edith said.

"No." Thomas half put out a hand, then let it fall to his side. "You'd best hear this too." He held out a sheet of paper. "I need your help."

CHAPTER 17

o. 43 Conduit Street was an elegant if anonymous terrace house of cream-colored stone set in a line of similar houses. But unlike many of those houses, it was in darkness. The moonlight emerging from behind the clouds gleamed off the walls but the windows were dark.

Julien scanned the building. "I suggest Harry and Kitty go in with Miss Lambton. Perhaps Mr. and Miss Schofield and Laura would come round the back with me. I'm sure we can find an alternative way in."

Thus keeping the young Schofields out of the way while also positioning Julien to take action from the outside. Kitty sent her husband an approving look.

"Is it safe?" Justine asked Harry and Kitty. "For you to come in with me?"

"The house is in darkness," Kitty said. "If anyone's waiting in the front hall, they're there to ambush you."

Justine gave a quick nod. "What about the door?"

"Presumably whoever sent the note left a way for you to get in," Harry said. "If not, both Kitty and I are quite capable of picking a lock."

But when Harry tried the door, it opened with well-oiled ease. The smell of lemon oil and the close air of a house that has been shut up greeted them as they stepped into the dark hall. And the faintest whiff of candles. Kitty caught a glow from the top of the stairs, not on the landing but perhaps from behind a door.

"Do come up." An imperious voice carried down the stairs, muffled by a door but carrying in a way that would have been effective onstage at the Tavistock. "Miss Lambton, do pray ask those who came with you to come out of hiding. There's no reason for them not to hear this. In fact, I am counting on their presence."

Even at this distance, the voice was unmistakable. Kitty cast a quick look at Harry. Surprise mingled with a sense of inevitability.

Harry put a hand on Justine's arm. "I don't think the danger is physical," he murmured.

They climbed the stairs in the shadows. A faint light came from a door ajar at the head of the stairs. Harry opened it, positioned to ward off an attack if necessary. Kitty could read the signs in his posture because she was ready to do the same herself."

"Don't be silly, Colonel Davenport," a crisp voice said from inside the room. "My methods have never run in that direction."

Harry stepped aside and held the door open to allow Kitty and Justine to precede him into the room. Keeping close to Justine, Kitty stepped into a siting room hung with French blue paper. Lady Shroppington, who surely had been in Emily Cowper's ballroom little more than an hour since, sat on a settee across from the door. A young woman with delicate features and smooth dark-blonde hair, gowned in crystal-beaded periwinkle crêpe, sat in a straight-backed chair at right angles to her.

"I'm glad you've all come," Lady Shroppington said. "Miss Schofield and I were beginning to despair of you."

Justine drew a sharp breath, her gaze going to Marianne Schofield. "Oh, thank goodness. Your family are so worried."

"Miss Lambton." Marianne pushed herself to her feet. "I had no notion—my family know I'm missing?"

"No, only Gerry and Sophia," Justine said. "Well, and Sally and Billy. But you know that."

"Dear god." Marianne Schofield put her hands to her face.

"I take it you summoned Miss Schofield here as well," Harry said to Lady Shroppington.

"You could put it that way." Lady Shroppington curled her right hand round the carved arm of the settee. "I haven't been close to my nephew's family of late. In truth, I thought I had washed my hands of them. But when it comes to the marriage of my great-nephew, I find I still take a certain interest. I was impelled to look into his betrothed's family."

"And you found a connection to trade," Marianne said in a level, well-modulated voice. "Hardly a great secret."

"If every family turned up their nose at a connection to trade, no one in the beau mode would be able to make an alliance. At first glance, your father's fortune indicated an enviable stability that could help the Thornsby family. But then I looked deeper. Which is why I asked you to meet me here tonight."

"You've scarcely asked me anything since I arrived," Marianne said.

"No. Because I was waiting for Miss Lambton to arrive as well. I knew she was on her way to London and I assumed she would find her way to the ball, but it took longer than I anticipated."

"You—" Justine took a step forwards. "You sent my father the letter in Cambridge? I don't even know who you are."

"Lady Shroppington," Harry said. "Thomas Thornsby's great-aunt. And a number of other things."

Lady Shroppington waved a hand between Marianne and Harry. "Miss Schofield, I assume you've met Colonel Davenport, given his association with my great-nephew." She glanced at Kitty. "Have you met Miss Schofield, Lady Carfax?"

"Not formally," Kitty said. "But after tonight, I confess I feel I know her. Miss Schofield."

Marianne inclined her head. "Lady Carfax."

Lady Shroppington pursed her lips. "I must say Colonel Davenport and Lady Carfax are not precisely the party I was expecting with Miss Lambton. Where have you hidden the others?"

"Here." Julien strolled through a side door (rather than the window, which Kitty was half expecting). Laura, Sophy, and Gerry followed him.

"Gerry! Sophy!" Marianne took a step towards them. "What are you doing here?"

"We could ask you the same," Gerry said. His gaze was a mix of relief and hard questions.

"You'd best all sit down." Lady Shroppington cast a glance round the room, which was tastefully furnished in giltwood and shades of blue, though Kitty now noticed a pile of Holland covers in one corner. "We won't be disturbed. Lady Hartlebury shut up the house and went off to Paris for the holidays. Supposedly for her health, though Paris seems an odd choice for that. I suspect the trip involves the Vicomte de Marais."

"Did she leave you a key?" Sophy asked. "Or can you pick locks too?"

Lady Shroppington, who most certainly could pick locks, sent Sophy a quelling glance. "That is hardly material at the moment." Her gaze moved from Marianne to Justine. "You've led very different lives. But you're both loyal to your families."

"I don't see why our families should have anything to do with this," Marianne said. Her gaze shot to Sophy, now perched on the window seat, and Gerry, hovering protectively between Sophy, Justine, and Marianne herself.

"And yet you came," Lady Shroppington said.

"Can you imagine I wouldn't when a threat to my family was

held over me?" Marianne said. "I imagine it's the same for Miss Lambton."

"Or perhaps you both feared the threat was to your own activities. That's an interesting subject, but my concern is for your fathers."

"Our fathers have scarcely seen each other since university," Justine said.

"Or so they give it out publicly." Lady Shroppington settled back on the settee with the air of a dramatist who has finally come to the denouement. Or an assassin closing in for the kill. "If they hadn't been in touch, it's quite a coincidence that they both ended up working for the French."

"What?" Justine surged out of her chair.

Marianne got to her feet more quietly, but her posture and tone were steely. "That's an outrageous allegation."

Gerry strode forwards. "You can't be serious."

"Honestly," Sophy said, "Papa isn't nearly interesting enough to be a spy."

"I imagine it seems so to his children," Lady Shroppington said. "But your father dealt information about British troop deployment to the French for years. And thanks to Miss Lambton's father, he had advance knowledge of the British victory at Waterloo that allowed him to make a fortune on the outcome."

"That's impossible," Justine said.

"Do you deny your father was in Paris at the time of Waterloo?" Lady Shroppington asked.

"Yes. No. He was there, but only because he'd gone to speak with fellow classicists and was trapped there when Bonaparte escaped and returned to power. He was staying quietly outside Paris. My father has no interests in any politics later than the fifth century. Maybe the fourth."

"It's a good cover. But at least one of the colleagues he was meeting with is a French agent."

Gerry took a step closer to Justine. Out of the corner of her eye, Kitty noted the door to the landing easing open.

Justine returned the fire in Lady Shroppington's gaze. "Even if that's true, it doesn't prove my father is one."

"Perhaps not. But there is the question of how else Miss Schofield's father got the information about Waterloo."

"Assuming he really was dealing with the French, from one of his spy colleagues?" Justine said.

"Which is precisely what happened." Raoul stepped into the room, followed by Mélanie and a tall man with sandy blond hair. "You can stop toying with all of us, Lady Shroppington. I will tell the truth, if necessary."

élanie followed Raoul and Theodore Schofield into the sitting room. They had heard Lady Shroppington's accusations from outside the door. Raoul had had to grip Schofield's arm to keep him from rushing into the room.

Lady Shroppington surveyed the three of them and let her gaze settle on Raoul. "Bold words, O'Roarke. I wonder what your wife thinks of your readiness to throw your hard-won safety away?"

"His wife never had any illusions our life was free of danger," Laura said.

Lady Shroppington glanced at her. "You're a strong-minded woman, Mrs. O'Roarke." Her voice was tinged with approval. "But even if you are willing to throw your comfortable life to the winds and risk having to flee, anything O'Roarke says will unravel a whole chain of secrets." She looked back at Raoul. "Are you prepared to drag Mrs. Rannoch into it as well?"

Raoul met Mélanie's gaze, his own level. "I think that's a decision for Mrs. Rannoch to make. But I'm quite sure of her answer."

"You know me well." Mélanie turned her gaze to Lady Shroppington. "I can understand your desire for revenge, but if this is your plan, you haven't read either of us very well."

"No?" Lady Shroppington's brows rose. "I thought you were concerned to protect your husband. But perhaps, as you say, I am misreading you."

Mélanie's throat tightened as though someone had jerked her necklace so the rubies and emeralds bit into her flesh. The desolation and panic of those moments when her past had been exposed and she and Malcolm had realized they had to flee to Italy washed over her, driving the breath from her lungs. But she wasn't the woman she'd been then. Her marriage to Malcom was different. She knew what they could survive. She knew how Malcolm would respond. And yet—

"I know my husband would lose all respect for me if I didn't protect an innocent person," she said.

"All of you have the most tiresome habit of putting so-called ideals ahead of practicality." Lady Shroppington said. "But I must say your tiresome ethics can be useful."

"Lady Shroppington—" Schofield said.

"Papa—" The girl who spoke must be Sophy, though both Gerry and Marianne had anguished gazes turned on their father.

Schofield turned to his children. "I never wanted you to hear this. But in the circumstances—"

He broke off as the door opened and Malcolm stepped into the room, followed by Thomas Thornsby and Edith.

"Oh, good," Lady Shroppington said. "I was hoping you'd arrive before we got to this part of it."

"Thornsby." Schofield looked as green as he had in the ballroom when Raoul first addressed him, but his gaze was steady. "I didn't want you to hear this, but I suppose it's inevitable you will, if the whole truth comes out. Some unfortunate aspects of my past have come to light. O'Roarke generously offered to come to my assistance, but there is no need. I'll come forwards myself." He looked at Lady Shroppington. "You can't imagine I'd let Lambton be dragged into this. Say what you will of me for betraying my country, but did you really think I'd betray a friend?"

"At the cost to your family?" Lady Shroppington said.

Schofield's gaze shot to his daughters and son.

"It's all right, Papa," Marianne said. "Just now I'm singularly proud of you."

"So am I," Gerry said.

"For perhaps the first time, we all agree," Sophy said.

Theodore Schofield's gaze lingered on his children. The space between them was set with mines that would no doubt shadow the future, if not explode it, but in that moment solidarity held the family together.

Marianne tore her gaze from her father and looked at Thomas. "In light of everything, I must offer to release you from our betrothal."

"On the contrary." Thomas took a step towards Marianne. "Tonight's events make me more determined than ever to stand by your family."

"I'm not sure our family deserves that," Sophy muttered.

"Soph!" Gerry jabbed her in the side.

"Well, we don't. Marianne does, though."

"You're a man of honor, Thomas," Marianne said. "But we made a bargain and this wasn't part of it."

Thomas moved to her side and took her hand. "It wasn't a bargain."

Mélanie felt Edith's absolute stillness. Her gaze was trained on Thomas as though the last few minutes had made her love him even more. Just at the moment she knew she had lost him.

Marianne's gaze fastened on Thomas's own. "I can't tell you what this means to me. But—"

She broke off as the door opened once again. Mélanie, who had heard the creak of the hinges an instant before Marianne reacted, turned to see Cordelia with Lucinda and Hubert Mallinson.

For the first time, some of the self-satisfaction left Lady Shroppington's face, though she quickly masked her uncertainty. "I wasn't expecting you. Though perhaps it's as well."

"My daughter and Lady Cordelia suggested I be here," Hubert said. "I understand there are some interesting accusations being made."

"Which you should hear," Lady Shroppington said. "For once, I applaud Lady Cordelia."

Theodore Schofield drew in his breath. Thomas turned to range himself beside Marianne, holding her hand.

"Yes, I've heard the accusations," Hubert said. "We were outside the door for some time. Interesting. But as it happens, I knew about Schofield all along." He glanced at Raoul. "I am desolated to tell you you were deceived, O'Roarke, but Schofield was a double working for me."

Silence gripped the room. Schofield stared at Hubert, seemingly as shocked as anyone.

"You can't seriously expect me to believe that," Lady Shroppington said.

"My dear Lady Shroppington," Hubert returned. "It isn't a question of what you believe, but of what I say."

Rage flared in her gaze. She turned to Raoul. "And you'll go along with this?"

"It explains a lot, don't you think?" Raoul said.

Lady Shroppington snorted. "In my day, intelligence was more hard-headed."

"One could argue that certain things in your past put the lie to that," Hubert said. He looked, Mélanie thought, distinctly satisfied with himself.

"Whatever I did," Lady Shroppington said, "none of it was for sentimental reasons."

"None of it?" Mélanie asked, their conversation at the ball sharp in her mind.

Lady Shroppington met her gaze for a moment. Even a spy can

drop their mask at moments. This was one of them. "Very little. But then, given the untidiness of the royal family in these matters, I don't know what we can expect." She looked at Schofield, disdain writ in her features, then looked from Hubert to Raoul. "Are you simply going to let him get away with it?"

Raoul looked from Schofield to his three children. The admiration of a few moments before had faded to confusion in the gazes of the young Schofields. As though a well-loved nursery book had proved to be a text written in unbreakable code. "I don't think he's got away with anything."

CHAPTER 19

Cordelia cast a bright glance round the ballroom. "It looks much like it did when we left. Save that a few more glasses of champagne have been consumed, and hairpins are sliding a trifle looser. That pine garland looks to have slithered several inches down that column. I imagine some stay laces have snapped too. I'm quite sure no one's noticed we were gone."

"How can you be sure?" Sophy asked.

Mélanie surveyed the ballroom. A waltz was playing. Couples were still swirling on the floor. Two ladies in front of them swept to the side, revealing scuff marks and spilled champagne on the floorboards. A blur of conversation, a bit more slurred than when they had left, sounded on all sides. To avoid notice, they had all slipped back into Emily Cowper's in small groups. She was standing by the French windows on the edge of the dance floor with Cordelia, Sophy, and Marianne. "I haven't moved among the beau monde nearly as long as Cordelia, but I can say that at this stage of a ball, no one is keeping track of who is in the ballroom, and there are all sorts of reasons for people to have disappeared."

Sophy's eyed widened. "You mean they think we were all having assignations in the shrubbery?"

"Or mending flounces in the retiring room," Cordelia said.

Sophy let her shawl slither lower on her shoulders. "I'd much rather be thought to be having an assignation. Well, depending on whom it was with."

"That makes all the difference," Cordelia agreed. She glanced round the ballroom again. "We should mingle."

Marianne gave a determined nod. Once they had re-entered Emily Cowper's, her composed façade had settled over her features again. She had a control that would serve her admirably as a spy. "It's all right. I know what I need to do."

"You must loathe me," Marianne Schofield said.

Edith started. She had been surprised when Marianne approached her on the edge of the dance floor, though not entirely shocked, given the events of the night. But she had been expecting a plea to keep the Schofields' family's secrets, not any reference to Thomas. "Why on earth would I? I'll admit to twinges of jealousy—well, I'll admit to more than twinges. But it's hardly your fault that you're the sort of woman Thomas could marry and I'm not. I'd be a poor creature if I disliked you for that."

Marianne gave a faint smile, though her gaze remained steady. "You're more generous than most people."

"I don't think so. I said I'm perfectly capable of jealousy. Even though I'm not at all sure I'd marry Thomas even if I could."

Marianne's perfectly arced brows rose. "You're in love with him."

"I—yes." It was, Edith realized, the first time she'd admitted it in so many words. What an odd person to be admitting it to.

"I didn't know," Marianne said. "That is, I knew Thomas wasn't in love with me, and I guessed there might have been someone else once, but until tonight I didn't realize it was someone who was still a part of his life. Someone he might have married."

Edith tugged at her shawl. Predictably, it was slithering to the floor. "That was never really a possibility."

"But it could have happened," Marianne said. "It's not as though you're married to someone else or far away or—"

"Dead?"

"Well, yes. That is a possibility when someone has a lost love."

"Thomas and I never even discussed marriage."

"But you must have—I mean, it must have occurred to you. To both of you."

"No. Yes, I suppose so, but mostly as something impossible that I didn't think I'd be very good at." Edith regarded Marianne. For all the other woman had been through this night, her gown still fell in precise folds, her gloves were barely creased, and her glossy blonde side curls framed her face with precision. "That was part of why I was jealous of you. Because you'll obviously make him an admirable wife. In all the ways I wouldn't."

"I don't see why you should assume that."

"You understand this world."

"You must as well. Forgive me, I don't know a great deal about you, but doesn't a governess have to understand it in order to instruct her pupils?"

"I suppose so." Edith remembered her days in the Wilton household. "But to the extent I did, it was only to realize how unsuited I am to that world."

"You're assuming I'm suited to it."

"Of course you are."

"Why of course?"

"You were going to Almack's and balls and you were presented at court. That's the sort of thing one does when looking for a husband."

"Or when one's parents are looking for a husband."

"So you don't want to get married either?"

"I—" Marianne fingered the sticks of her fan. "I always thought I did. It was the life I was brought up for. Nothing else seemed possible." She frowned, watching Edith. "You said you aren't sure you'd marry Thomas even if you could. But you said you love him."

"I—" Edith drew a breath and swallowed. "Yes."

"I should have thought that was the one reason to marry someone. Well, not the only one, but—"

"But marriage means so much more, doesn't it? I mean, it's a bit like signing on for a profession, only if one's a woman one's husband's life determines the profession. What if one falls in love with a politician but doesn't want to be a politician's wife? Come to think of it, I think that's rather what happened to Mélanie Rannoch, but she seems to have managed. But for most people—"

"I suppose if one loves someone, one is supposed to want to help them succeed."

"Yes, but at the cost of one's own dreams? Suppose it means having to go across the Continent on a diplomatic posting, or give endless boring parties, or simply not have time for one's own work."

Marianne closed her arms over her chest. "I never thought about having my own work."

"Most women don't. That is, I suppose most women take it for granted they have to go into service or work on the farm or in a factory or something. But most women of fortune don't. I became a governess because it was quite clear I had to do something to make a living. And I couldn't bear the thought of marrying for money."

"Like Mr. Thornsby." Marianne's gaze was steady.

"Yes. No. Well, in a way. But he has his sisters to think about. Perhaps if I were really a good sister, I'd have married Mr. Tompkins the brewer and supported my own brothers and sisters. But I'm not as self-sacrificing as Thomas."

"That's an interesting way of putting it."

"He's a good man."

"Yes, I don't doubt that he is." Marianne's fingers dug into her pristine gloves. "That's one of the reasons I accepted him. I thought we could deal well together." She cast a quick glance at Edith. "I wasn't in love with him, I didn't expect to find love, but even if marriage is a bargain, that doesn't mean one doesn't want to find someone one *likes*."

"Yes, I can see that. But why were you so convinced you'd never fall in love? I thought that was the dream of young girls in their first season."

Marianne's mouth curled with what seemed uncharacteristic irony. "Having spent endless balls and nights at Almack's and in the retiring rooms at the palace, I'd say the dream of most girls making their debut is to have a successful season with an engagement as a sort of prize at the end of it. Quite independent of the gentleman involved, except in so far as he lends one consequence. And little or no thought to the life one will have after one leaves St. George's, Hanover Square, and finishes the cake from Gunter's."

Edith considered Marianne Schofield as she might a text that yielded unexpected information that put a previous thesis in doubt. "That sounds very apt. Though rather more jaded than what I'd have expected from you."

The irony in Marianne's smile deepened, along with a touch of regret. "I may not be a scholar, but I pride myself on being at least passingly observant. I wasn't immune to the excitement of the game, but I did recognize that it was a game. And I retained enough sense to have some thought for the life I'd have after the game ended." Her brows drew together. "At least, so I told myself. But now it seems absurd that I ever thought Thomas and I could have a good life together."

"That's the first time I've heard you call him Thomas," Edith said.

Marianne's mouth twisted, almost with regret. "Perhaps I see him more as a person now. As someone with his own wants and regrets. It seems rather shameful that I thought we could be happy together when it clearly conflicted with so much of what he wanted."

"It wasn't your job to know what Thomas wanted," Edith said in a quiet voice.

"Wasn't it? Isn't it the job of both partners in a marriage to have some care for what the other wants? How can a marriage start successfully when the partners aren't paying heed to that?"

"I doubt most people have the least heed what their marriage partner wants when they make their vows."

"Yes, so do I. That makes it all the worse."

Edith regarded Thomas's betrothed. "What do *you* want?"

"I don't know. I thought I wanted a stable family and my own household. It's not just that I've never had to work like you do. I've never had an interest like you do. Or like Thomas does, I suppose. It must be rather splendid to have something you're that consumed by."

"Yes." Edith felt herself smile. "It's a reason to get up in the morning. It's something to keep one's thoughts interesting, even through the drudgery of life." She hesitated. "When I first heard of the betrothal, I wondered how that would work. If Thomas could be happy with someone who I assumed wasn't interested in classics."

"It's a fair question."

"Yes, but then it occurred to me that it would probably be quite a relief to have someone who ordered dinner at the right time and didn't forget to have the linens changed or order fresh flowers— not to mention dusting the vase. I'm not cut out to run a household."

"Perhaps you need a good housekeeper. And a good nursemaid."

"Thomas and I wouldn't have had the funds for much of a staff. And if I had children, I'd want to raise them myself. They're time consuming, but they're quite interesting. Far more interesting than I realized when I became a governess. But I still worry about—"

"About how you'd manage without funds?"

"No. I'm used to not having a lot. I think even Thomas could manage if he had his books. But he wouldn't be able to help his family, and that would eat at him."

"But you said you weren't sure you'd marry anyway. Because—?"

"Because I'd worry about how much of myself I'd be giving up."

"I'm not sure I know enough of myself to think about what I'd be giving up."

"You've never been in love?"

Marianne folded her arms and gripped her elbows. "No."

But Edith caught a flicker in Marianne's gaze. "Never? Mind you, I can understand not falling in love at all—before Thomas, I never thought I would. But then, the whole thought of marriage seemed rather horrid to me. If you always assumed you'd marry, I would think the idea of falling in love would be rather appealing."

Marianne straightened her shoulders. "My dear Miss Simmons. Surely you realize in our world, marriage and love don't go hand in hand."

"You sound like Lady Shroppington. But surely if you expected to marry, you at least considered falling in love with the person?"

"Perhaps I never met such a person."

"And you did fall in love, but not with anyone you could hope to marry? I can understand that. That's rather what I did, against all my better instincts. That's what Thomas did. But you have a fortune. Did it occur to you to defy your parents? I mean, I know the prospect of being poor isn't appealing, but you look like you have resolve, and I doubt your parents would cut you off without a shilling. Unless he's married already? That would be a conundrum. Oh dear, I shouldn't be prattling on. It's none of my business."

"No." Marianne put out a hand and then let it fall. "We're being frank with each other. Which is a great relief. It seems wrong to deny it all, somehow. But please understand, there's no way the person in question and I can be together. It's folly to think about it. So I realized I simply had to get on with my life. Only I didn't consider that that might mean making a hash of someone else's life. Thomas deserves better."

"Thomas can take of himself."

Marianne looked sharply at Edith.

"I mean it. I love him, but he's a grown man who's made his own choices. Those choices may not have made me happy, but I understand them. And Thomas would be the first to say he has to live by them."

"Yes, but I don't want him to. That is, I don't want to be part of someone's settling."

"Even though you're settling yourself?"

"But I'm not. Thomas could marry you. I don't have that option."

"And that's a reason to settle for something else? Forgive me, I don't know the reasons you can't marry the person you love, but Thomas couldn't marry me without abandoning his family, at least as he sees it, which is a fairly insuperable barrier. And if you marry without love, the man you marry will be doing the same. Unless he's in love with you, which seems rather worse."

"Yes. I suppose it does."

"So you want someone who's ready to make a bargain? That's defines Thomas perfectly."

"You don't want him to walk away from the betrothal? I should think—"

"That I'd want him to choose me?" Edith ruthlessly suppressed the unbidden moment of joy that had coursed through her when Marianne had offered to release Thomas. And the sinking desolation she'd felt when it was clear that Marianne's predicament had only made Thomas even more determined to honor the betrothal. "That sounds very splendid in a novel or play and would make for a wonderful scene, but in practice I fear it would be distinctly challenging. And I don't think anyone can properly build happiness on making others unhappy."

"Well, then. I can't build it on making my family unhappy."

Edith felt herself frown. "I think that's a bit different. I mean, Thomas's sisters wouldn't have dowries and his parents wouldn't be able to repair the roof. That's a bit different from one's family's simply wanting one to live a different life."

"My mother's wanted this since I was a baby."

"And it's your job to secure it for her?"

"Not just for her. For my sisters and brothers and their children—my family are intertwined with my choices. Just like for Thomas. Are my goals less important than his?"

"I suppose when the goal is financial security, it seems different."

"But my sisters and brothers would have different options in life." Marianne regarded Edith. "Do you have sisters and brothers?"

"Two younger sisters, one elder brother, two younger."

"If one of them could have made an alliance so you wouldn't have had to become a governess, wouldn't you have wanted that?"

Edith forced herself to examine possible scenarios. "I won't deny being a governess had its challenges. I won't claim not to be glad to be done with it—much pleasanter to teach and help run a school. But I'd have felt beastly being indebted to my sisters and brothers. And in some ways I'd have had less freedom. I mean, as a governess, I might have only had one day off, but at least it was my decision what to do with it. My mother would have had no end of strictures on how I should behave every minute of the day."

Marianne tilted her head to the side. "Perhaps you should tell Thomas."

"What?"

"That his sisters might be happier if he didn't sacrifice himself on the altar of family duty."

"His sisters aren't me."

"Perhaps they'd be more like you if they had the chance."

Edith bit back an instinctive denial and thought of what she knew about Thomas's sisters. Which wasn't much. And she had tended to dismiss them as being like—well, like the sort of woman she had believed Marianne Schofield to be.

"If they were your sisters, isn't that what you'd want?" Marianne asked.

"Is that what you'd want for your sisters?" Edith counted.

"I think so. Now." Marianne drew a breath. "I think perhaps I'm growing up."

"And for yourself?"

"I think—I don't want to be the cause of anyone else's unhappiness."

"Including your own?"

"I'm not sure that's possible," Marianne said.

CHAPTER 20

"It looks as though everything's going well." Lucinda stopped beside Mélanie in the salon off the ballroom. "Julien brought us in through the garden, up the service stairs. Gerry Schofield and Justine Lambton and me. And Kitty. It was quite a lark. I wish more Mallinsons were like him."

"I imagine your father would say thank goodness they aren't. And yet, while Julien is unique, in some ways I think he's very much a Mallinson."

"Yes, so do I. But I don't think either Julien or Papa would like it if we said so." Lucinda took a sip of champagne. "Papa was quite helpful tonight. It was a nice change."

"We owe him a great deal," Mélanie said.

"Do you really mean that?"

"Certainly." Which didn't discount the fact that Hubert Mallinson could still be a formidable enemy.

Lucinda smiled, then frowned as she took another sip of champagne. "The only sad part of the evening is that Marianne and Thomas Thornsby seem more betrothed than ever. I was quite hopeful for a moment, when she offered to release him from the betrothal."

"Thomas would never have accepted her offer. Not when she was in trouble."

"No, I suppose not. But it leaves them in worse straits than ever. And I can't help feeling I should be able to fix it."

Mélanie put a hand on Lucinda's arm. "You can't fix everything for your friends, Lucy."

"Yes, but I'm not going to stand by and watch them blunder into a hideous mistake. There must be something we can do."

"Ultimately, Thomas and Marianne are the ones who have to make the choice."

"Yes, I suppose so. But that doesn't mean—" Lucinda looked round the room. "Have you seen Charlotte?"

"You're very fortunate to be able to be in the Classicists' Society," Justine said. "That is, I know it's hard work not good fortune, but—"

"No, a part of it is good fortune." Cordelia smiled at the younger woman. She and Harry had invited Justine to stay with them for a few days. They were sending off an express to reassure her father, though Justine assured them she had covered her tracks. "Which I didn't recognize enough at first."

"But you've always liked classics."

"Oh yes. Though after I made my debut I got distracted by a lot of other things. Granted classics were something Harry and I shared. One of the few things at first, I confess. But I'd have thought the Classicists' Society had little to offer beside a ball." Cordelia glanced at the crowd still on the dance floor, draining the last dregs from the evening. She still enjoyed balls but many nights she'd choose the Classicists' Society.

"So you go now because of your husband?"

"No. That is, classics was always something Harry and I could talk about. I used to laugh at how he would barricade himself with his books, but sometimes I'd come home from a ball and help him with a bit of translation and realize that was actually the most fun part of my evening. Then there were other challenges we faced. But classics was something we had in common."

"Is that why you like it now? Because of your husband?"

"No. Yes. That is, I love that it's something we share. But that isn't why I'm a classicist. It took a long time for me to call myself a classicist. And to realize that I really was one. If I were just helping Harry, I don't think I'd use the word."

"I don't think you're just helping him at all. I've read the papers you've written. They're splendid. And I thought that before I knew you'd written them. Or who you were. I mean not that—"

"No, I quite understand." Cordelia smiled. "I could seem like a society fribble."

"Not that. But I'd never met anyone like you. I've never been to a London ball until tonight. We meet lots of young men from the ton but not so many women. Not that there's any reason one shouldn't be able to enjoy balls and society and be a classical scholar. Or anything else. It's silly to think that being serious about something means one can't enjoy frivolous things." Justine looked down at her borrowed gown. "I only borrowed this dress so I could fit in, but I confess I quite like it. Like getting to pretend to be someone else."

"Or explore a different part of yourself."

Justine wrinkled her nose. "I think the dressing up might be fun." She looked down at the glass in her hand. "And the champagne and music and even the dancing. I don't think I'd be very good at flirting though."

"Oh, I don't think anyone thinks they're good at flirting."

"Surely you do. Did?"

"Possibly now when I'd only do it in the service of an investigation and my husband would know perfectly well what I was doing. Before—" Cordelia thought back to herself at seventeen. Suddenly aware of new powers and eager to put them to the test.

But soon she'd been too obsessed with George to have interest in others. And once George married and she emerged from her grief she'd been too angry and bitter to do more than flirt out of a reflexive desire not to be alone. It had been the same after she married Harry, though it had perhaps also been an attempt to get her husband's attention, something she hadn't realized until years later. And after her affair with George and separation from Harry, it had been an attempt to distract herself with sensation. And for some sort of connection, even if a fleeting one. While living defiantly down to people's expectations of her. But perhaps there had been a certain power in knowing she could win at the game. "Perhaps at times," she said. "But half the time it feels one's making a hopeless muddle of it."

"Is it easier to be in love?"

"I think that's worse perhaps. Because one takes it more seriously."

"Yes, I can see that. Not that I've—But I can imagine."

"On the other hand," Cordelia said, "it's far more worth the effort. That is, it can be if it's the right person. Which of course one doesn't know. At least I didn't for the longest time."

Justine's gaze flickered across Cordelia's face, at once hesitant and curious. In the end the scholar won out. "So when you met your husband—"

"Oh when I met Harry I couldn't see it at all."

"You didn't find it easy to flirt with him?"

"It never would have occurred to me to flirt with Harry." Cordelia stopped short because he was one of the few men about whom that was true. "I think that was part of why he seemed safe to me. Only he wasn't safe at all. Which is probably a good thing because I don't think love is very safe."

"Never?"

"Well—when I'm with Harry now I do feel safe. But loving someone is always a risk. Because you can get hurt. And it took me a long time to admit to myself—or Harry or anyone else—that I was in love."

"And if you hadn't married him, you might not have realized you wanted to be a classicist."

That brought Cordelia up short as well. "Very likely not. It's amazing where life takes one. But I think you're going about it much more sensibly. Much more the way I'd like to see my daughters go about it. Being a classicist first and being secure in that and then finding someone to love."

"I haven't found someone to love."

"No? Perhaps not yet. But you seem as though you'll be quite sensible about it when you do."

"I thought you said love wasn't sensible."

Cordelia felt herself smile. "Caught. It often isn't. I don't think it ever feels sensible. But some people do manage to fall in love with a sensible choice. Perhaps they have more of a sense of what they want."

Thomas was on the edge of the dance floor when Marianne approached him. He always felt a bit awkward when he realized he had to have private conversation with her, but despite—or perhaps because of—the events of the night, the awkwardness seemed to have eased. He held out a hand to her. "Shall we dance again?"

"I don't think that's necessary, do you?" Marianne said. "No one seems to be gossiping."

"That isn't the only reason to dance."

Marianne paused, close enough for private conversation but not close enough to touch him. "You're a good man, Thomas. I always knew that, but I saw it even more tonight. I can't tell you how much it means that you were willing to stand by me."

"No man of honor would have done otherwise."

"Then there are few men of honor in London society."

"Whatever your father may have done shouldn't reflect on you."

"It can't help but hang over our family, but that's something Gerry and Sophy and I have to sort out with him." She folded her hands together. "You're a remarkable man, Thomas. I thought we could be happy. And perhaps had circumstances been different we might have been. But I see now how selfish I was to see the situation only from my own perspective. And I see the impossibility of happiness being built on denying the happiness of others."

"I never said—"

"No. You didn't need to. I saw you looking at her tonight."

Denial would have been fruitless. He could tell that from Marianne's gaze. And denial seemed like a denial of who he was. "It was over," he said, his voice hoarse. "Before I offered for you. It was never a real possibility."

"But that doesn't make the feelings go away. I could see that tonight. And you're not the only one for whom that's true."

His gaze locked on her own. Impossible to question her past. And yet—"I'm sorry," he said. "I begin to think I never really knew you at all."

Marianne smiled. "We probably knew each other as well as most of the married couples in this ballroom. Which is to say not well at all. I was so busy keeping my own secrets I didn't make nearly enough of an attempt to get to know you."

"I never should have offered—"

"I never should have accepted. We both did what we thought was required of us. But the good thing is there is still time to fix it. As a man of honor, I am sure you will not attempt to hold me when I tell you I wish to cry off from our engagement. And in the spirit of honesty, you can't tell me you aren't more than a bit relieved."

For a moment, the relief was dizzying. As though he could

breathe for the first time in weeks. "I hope you won't take it as offense."

She smiled. Perhaps the most genuine smile he had ever seen from her. "On the contrary. For once I believe our feelings are completely in agreement."

CHAPTER 21

*R*aoul found Marianne Schofield near the French windows to the balcony, brows drawn, gaze fixed beyond the glass. "Not thinking of leaving again, are you?" he asked.

"What? Oh, no. Just reflecting on a conversation I had." She settled the folds of her shawl over her shoulders. "The news will be all over London soon. Mr. Thornsby and I have agreed we would not suit."

"Ah. I should say I am sorry. But I think perhaps you will both be happier?"

She met his gaze, her own uncharacteristically direct. "I think so."

Raoul nodded. They turned, both looking out the glass at the glow of the colored lamps from the garden below. "Laura and I talked to Sally and Billy tonight," he said.

"It was unpardonable of me to have involved them."

"On the contrary. They're concerned for you, but they obviously relished the adventure and have shown great mettle." Raoul hesitated. "I would suggest you return the music box as soon as possible."

Marianne's gaze shot to his face.

"It's none of my affair now the investigation is concluded," he said. "But it does lead me to think you at first thought Lady Shroppington had summoned you over something other than your father's past. And that you thought the confrontation would not allow you to return home."

Marianne held his gaze, her own steady. She had a self-possession that would do a seasoned agent credit.

Raoul dug a hand into his pocket. "I also thought you might like this back." He held out the earring.

Marianne went from still to carved in ice. "That isn't mine."

"Not originally, but I think you dropped it tonight. I suspect it was a keepsake. Perhaps you had it in your reticule and pulled it out to look at before you left the garden."

Her stillness cracked. "How can you—"

"It's only a theory, based on pieces I've put together. And as I said, it's no business of mine to intrude now that we've established that you're safe. But if you'll permit me to say so, I fell in love with my wife at a time when we couldn't be together without scandal. At the start, a part of me felt I should avoid any entanglement at all for her sake. And to protect my own feelings perhaps. We tried to keep it secret, but in the end we lived together despite the scandal. Which could be called appallingly selfish on my part. Eventually we were able to marry. But even if we hadn't been, I wouldn't regret snatching what we had together."

Marianne reached out and took the earring. "You had a happy ending. There aren't happy endings for everyone."

"I'd say there aren't endings. No one knows what lies ahead. And it depends how you define happy. But for myself, I can say it would be worth it. Even if we'd had to keep it secret forever. We'd still have had each other."

CHAPTER 22

"I returned the earring to Marianne Schofield," Raoul said.

Laura looked up from tucking the covers round Clara in her cradle. "So she could give it back to Charlotte Wilcox?"

"If she chooses to." Raoul shrugged off his evening coat. "I suspect it was a keepsake."

"I wondered about that as well." Laura twitched a fold of Clara's blanket smooth. "Sally said the earring belonged to Miss Wilcox, but Miss Wilcox was wearing blue tonight with pearl earrings and she wasn't missing either. I made sure to look when we returned to the ball. And then there's the music box and the papers it contains. Did Marianne Schofield admit it?"

"Not in so many words. But she didn't deny it."

"Damnably difficult for them, even now she's ended the betrothal." By the time they'd left Emily Cowper's, they'd all heard about Marianne and Thomas's called-off betrothal. Thomas had asked for their help spreading the news discreetly. "I hope they can find a way to make it work." Laura glanced at the nursery where her older daughter Emily was asleep, then looked down at Clara, thinking of all the possible challenges in their future.

148

"I told Miss Schofield what we have would be worth it even if it had had to remain secret."

Laura smiled at him. "Which it would be. Though as I recall, you were inclined to worry."

"About what I was putting you through? I could hardly do otherwise." Raoul moved to the armchair by the banked fire. "Laura?"

Laura turned from the cradle. Her husband was watching her, his face unexpectedly intent. "What, darling?"

"Do you ever wonder what your life would be like if you hadn't married me?"

Laura crossed the room and perched on the arm of Raoul's chair. "Are you wondering what your life would be like if you hadn't married me?"

"Not in the least. I know perfectly well it would be far less than it is now."

"You'd be able to spend more time in Spain."

"I don't want to spend more time in Spain."

"Never?"

"I may feel guilty. It's not the same thing." He laced his fingers through her own. "Mélanie asked me. She said Edith Simmons asked her. That Edith was wondering about what would have happened if she had been able to marry Thomas."

"Oh, well. That doesn't surprise me. I like Thomas, but he's far more conventional than you or Malcolm. It would be a question of if he tried to change Edith, or if she could change him."

"You don't think he could change her?"

"Not Edith. But he could make her miserable. I can see her not wanting to run the risk. Edith's quite brilliant. And quite self-possessed."

"So are you."

Laura looked down into her husband's gray eyes. "I didn't want to marry again."

"Yes, I know."

"I wouldn't have married anyone but you."

"That doesn't necessarily answer the question."

"I was only just beginning to forge a life of my own."

"Which might be all the more reason to wonder about the life you'd have had without me."

"You didn't stop me from forging a life. From being a writer and a teacher. I was already a mother." She'd had Emily before she married Raoul, for all Raoul was now Emily's father. But without him she wouldn't have Clara. Her gaze went to the cradle. "I can't imagine not having Clara."

"Nor can I."

"You have a way of filling up space, Raoul. I can't imagine the world without you."

He gave a wry smile. "That might make you more inclined to wonder what you'd have if you had—more space."

"I don't want more space." She slid off the arm of the chair into his lap. She remembered the moment she'd first glimpsed him, in the Rannochs' salon in Paris. She hadn't known who he was, but his eyes had burned with life. "I want what I wanted from the moment we met in Paris."

"What?"

"You."

Kitty closed the door of the guest bedroom at the Rannochs'. Bet and Sandy had got all the children to sleep in the night nursery by the time they returned from Emily Cowper's. They hadn't been planning to stay the night, but the Rannochs had two guest bedrooms, as well as dressing rooms to accommodate Edith and Justine Lambton. It was hardly the first time Kitty and Julien and Cordelia and Harry and their children had stayed in Berkeley Square at the last minute. This bedchamber already felt almost as though it was theirs. "I was enjoying a mission that was free of the past," she said, pulling the door to. "Folly perhaps to think we'd have one. Lady Shroppington was bound to reappear at some point."

Julien watched her, halfway across the room, the light from the candle he'd carried upstairs sliding over his face. "You're being very forbearing, sweetheart."

"About what, in particular?"

"Putting up with everything I put you through. Particularly in October."

October. When the defense had begun in the queen's case in the trial before the Lords. When she had stabbed Julien in the arm to stop him from strangling Alistair Rannoch. "You haven't changed, Julien."

He set the candle down on the night table and watched a drop of wax plop into the pewter candle holder. "Yes, that rather seems to be the problem."

"I mean the events of last October didn't change you. You've changed immeasurably from the man I met. I've changed as well." The brittle woman she'd been then could never have even imagined settling into partnership as she had. "But I've always known the man you are." Kitty walked up to her husband and slid her arms round him. "Nothing you could do could change the way I feel about you."

"I think we tested that enough in October. I'm not sure we could survive another." His mouth twisted. "Whatever I did, I always told myself I did it out of reason. I was in control of what I did, what lines I crossed. I might question my choices, but I never doubted that they were reasoned choices." He looked down at her. "I never lost control until I met you, you know. In a number of ways."

"Julien—"

"No, it's true. For good or ill. If you don't let yourself care, there's nothing to lose control over. When I heard Alistair had talked to Leo—I've never known such rage. I wanted to protect him."

Kitty held her husband's gaze. Rare to see such uncertainty in those blue eyes. "You must know what it means to me that you love Leo that much."

"I'm muddling still, you know," he said. "To be part of a family."

"Oh, so am I." She tightened her arms round him. "But the remarkable thing is we are one."

He kissed her hair. "It was a year ago, you know."

"What was?"

"When we spent the holidays together. When I felt impelled to spend a season I thought I loathed with you and the children."

"I remember. I didn't let myself admit how much that meant to me. You shocked me by looking round my rooms and saying they felt like home."

He gave a crooked smile. "My darling, that may be the first home I've ever known."

MÉLANIE CLOSED the door to the night nursery. "Stupid to let myself think it was over."

"Lady Shroppington?" Malcolm looked up from petting Berowne, who was curled up on their bed. "I don't think it will ever be over for her."

"Nor do I." Mélanie released the door handle and rubbed her arms, bare above her long gloves. "But I meant my past. Or if I didn't think it was over, I let myself push it aside. We're always going to be dealing with this."

"Undoubtedly," Malcolm said. "That was always clear."

Mélanie shot a look at him.

Malcolm kept his gaze on her while he scratched Berowne behind the ears. "It's part of who you are. Part of who I am now too. Part of why we're together. For which I'm immeasurably

152

grateful." He perched on the edge of the bed. "I said we had to get past it. That doesn't mean I ever thought we could ignore it. That doesn't mean we have to be afraid of it."

"And we've learned to live with it as a family," Mélanie said. "But I was so busy focusing on us I didn't give much heed to how it could impact people we don't even know."

"It's not just you, sweetheart. It's Raoul. Julien. Archie. We're all living with it."

"But Lady Shroppington was using me to get back at you."

"And Raoul. Possibly Raoul more. He's the one Alistair hates."

She moved to stand in front of him, meeting his gaze in the flickering light of the candles they'd carried upstairs. "I'm always going to be putting you at risk, Malcolm."

"You're worth it."

"Darling!"

"It's true. And a better answer than denying the issues, don't you think? I was a bit too inclined to do that at first, as I recall."

"No. Yes. But now you're—"

He ran his fingers through Berowne's fur. "What?"

"Not taking it seriously."

The candle flame jumped in his eyes. "Sweetheart. I'll always take it seriously. But we have to live our lives. Right now we're safe. We have less to worry about than Edith and Thomas."

Mélanie frowned. Edith had been bright-eyed and determined when she retired to the guest dressing room. But the turmoil had been there at the back of her eyes. "At least Marianne broke the betrothal. I was looking at all of them tonight and thinking how different it is for us."

"Well, yes. Little as we knew each other, I'd say we knew each other better than Thomas and Marianne did. Even though you were spying on me."

"That may be true, but that's not what I meant. I meant now. We can cheerfully ignore society. I can write plays and even appear onstage. We aren't invited a few places, but we could go out in society far more than we wish to if we put our minds to it."

"I'd prefer to go out even less."

"Quite. Even if we weren't invited anywhere, we'd be quite happy with the friends we have. But it's because we have a fortune. Because you have a fortune."

"Alistair's fortune. Which isn't really rightfully mine at all."

"Define 'rightfully.' In any case, even if you gave everything up that you inherited from Alistair, you have plenty from Arabella. We're never going to have to fear not living in comfort, to put it mildly. That insulates us from so much. Thomas has to play the social game because it's his only way of providing for his family."

"Which is damnably unfair. Even as a member of the beau monde, Thomas is still caught in this game."

"You could say he's trapped by conventions, but there isn't an obvious answer for him." Mélanie pushed herself up on the edge of the bed beside her husband. "Do you think they'd be happy?"

"Thomas and Edith?" Malcolm frowned. An odd relief shot through her at the fact that he hadn't given the easy, obvious answer of 'of course.' "Edith needs to be able to fly free. If Thomas could understand that—not just understand it, but act on it—I think they'd have a decent shot of it working. If not, it could end in flames."

"You're remarkable, Malcolm."

"I'm damned lucky you stayed with me as long as you did before it dawned on me you loathed the life we were living."

"I didn't loathe it in the least. I quite enjoyed it some of the time." She rubbed Berowne's head. "Too much of the time, perhaps. Talking of people who live a life of privilege while wanting to change the system."

"But it was never a life you'd have chosen and it was a waste of your talents." He looked at her for a moment. "I've never quite said it, but you must have felt trapped."

She met his gaze. "I never felt trapped being your wife, darling. I did at times feel trapped in my role. But that's being a spy."

He reached out and slid his hand behind her neck. "Even when you stopped being a spy, you were playing a role."

"Well, yes. I couldn't tell you the truth."

"That's not what meant. You were playing at being a political and diplomatic hostess."

"I wasn't *playing* at it. I took it seriously. I even enjoyed it."

"But it wasn't the life you'd have chosen. You were trying to be something you'd never have chosen on your own because you thought it was what I wanted. Isn't that just what you fear for Edith?"

"Yes. That is, no. It is what I fear for Edith, but I never—"

He rubbed his thumb against her neck. "Sweetheart. You can't tell me you were being yourself."

"I was—" She swallowed. Malcolm was smiling, but his gaze scoured her face, seeking honesty. Malcolm was the first to acknowledge the shifting nature of truth, but that didn't stop him from seeking it. "I thought it was the life we needed to live if we were to be together. Lots of people shape their lives to the people they marry."

"My point precisely."

"But I was happy."

"Edith might be happy as well."

"Maybe. But I think she'd get restless faster—" Mélanie bit back the words.

"Faster than you did?"

"Yes. No. Don't put words in my mouth, darling." She set her hands on his shoulders. "I wanted to be with you. I was willing to do what I needed to to make it work."

His gaze settled on her face. He was still smiling but his eyes had gone serious. "My point precisely, sweetheart. You shouldn't have to sacrifice yourself to make your marriage work. Ultimately I don't think it would have."

"I'd never have—"

"You might have started to resent me. Pardonably."

"Darling—"

"It's a delicate balancing act, forging a life together. I don't think one should ever assume nothing can shake the balance. The damnable thing is I never saw it. Worse, I never even thought there was something to see."

"If you mean—"

"No, not your being a spy. That you might want to be something other than a political wife. I knew you were brilliant at it. I knew you loved politics. But I never thought about what you might want on your own."

"Probably because very few people think that way about wives."

He raised a brow. "Yes, but I'm supposed to be aware of those issues. In theory, I knew all about the compromises women make. In practice, I simply let my wife build her life round me and didn't notice."

"I wouldn't—"

"Tell me you never thought that."

"No."

"Mel—"

A conversation she'd had with her friend Manon Caret echoed in her mind. The moments she brought Malcolm coffee, edited his speeches, made his life easier in countless ways she doubted he even noticed. "I never did anything I didn't want to do. That includes spying on you and marrying you. And most important, stopping spying and staying married to you."

"Clever, sweetheart. Answer a difficult question by answering another question entirely."

"All right, yes," she said. "But I could hardly expect you to notice anything was amiss. I could hardly expect anything different. After all, you were—"

"A British gentleman. You've hung that epithet round my neck so many times."

She tilted her head back but her smile wasn't quite as playful as she intended. "All right, I confess I didn't give you credit for being as broadminded as you are. But only because it was hard to grasp just how extraordinary you are."

"Flatterer."

"It's true."

"So you fell in love with me, thinking I was narrow-minded and too self-involved to appreciate what my wife was going through."

"Don't put words in my mouth, darling. I wouldn't possibly have fallen in love with anyone of the sort." She linked her hands behind his neck and looked into his eyes. "Marriage is challenging enough. A shocking invasion of privacy, as I've said. It's a bit much to expect one's partner to be fully aware of what one needs in life."

"Don't let me off the hook."

"I wasn't. I'm sure there's a lot I wasn't aware of."

"You've always been far more aware than I was in our marriage. As a spy, you had to be."

"A palpable hit."

"Sweetheart. I can't claim to know a great deal about marriage. I'm still not sure I'm suited to it. I doubt ours would work so well if you weren't so good at it. But I do know it hasn't a hope in hell if it isn't equal."

"A lot of marriages don't have hope then."

"Well, it doesn't have a hope of being what it should be."

Berowne rolled on his back and kneaded her leg, protesting the lack of attention. Mélanie rubbed his stomach. "Which brings us back to Thomas and Edith. Do you think they could be happy?"

"I think they might be happy. I also think Edith could be happy on her own. Possibly happier. I'm not sure. I'd hate to see her limited. I hate the idea that I've limited you."

"You haven't. I have so many things with you I'd never have

had without you. Our lives take unexpected turns, as Cordy once said. There's no sense in comparing it to the life you might have had otherwise. You'd have been a different person. We'd have both been different people."

"Immeasurably less happy, in my case. But yes."

"But the person you'd have become might have quite liked the life he had. Which isn't to say—Malcolm, you know I'm happy. And don't worry, there's a lot I'm planning to achieve. That I might not have dreamt of if I weren't the person I am now." She leaned over Berowne and kissed him. "That's one thing one learns as a spy. There are always more layers to uncover."

EPILOGUE

"I used to hate Christmas." Julien looked up from attaching a wooden wheel that had come off the new carriage Timothy had received for Christmas the day before. "Growing up, because it was a day I had to spend with my family. Odd how one's appreciation of it changes as one's family changes."

"I used to ignore it." Raoul refilled Julien's cup of mulled wine. "Except for when I was on a mission. And then suddenly one finds one has people one wants to spend it with."

"That sounds distinctly sentimental, sweetheart," Laura said.

Raoul grinned and refilled her cup. "I'm feeling sentimental. Whatever traditions one follows, midwinter is a time to gather with those one cares about."

Julien took a sip of mulled wine while jiggling the wheel with his other hand. "Careful, O'Roarke, I think you just said you cared about me."

Raoul settled back on the sofa beside Laura. "And it wasn't even a slip of the tongue."

Mélanie looked round the library. Their friends and family were gathered, and more would soon be arriving. The revelry of Christmas had caught even those like her for whom the holiday

159

had never meant a great deal. And the enthusiasm, fueled by the children's glee, had spilled over into Boxing Day. Which had a mellow glow she almost enjoyed even more. Nothing like basking in the sense one had met the children's expectations. She looked towards the fireplace, where an elaborate world was set up of the wooden castle from several years ago (which had gone to Italy with them), a new puppet theatre, and a variety of dolls and wooden and stuffed animals. An elaborate performance was in progress, with Sandy joining in. Bet was reading a new book to Clara and Genny, though they seemed more interested in wrapping ribbons round Berowne, who was putting up with it for the moment.

"I wonder whom Lady Shroppington is spending the holidays with," Cordelia said.

"I doubt Alistair," Harry said. "Not because we don't know where he is. Because I'm not sure either of them wants to be in each other's company at present."

"Do you think she meant to seek you out at Emily Cowper's ball?" Cordelia asked Mélanie. "Before everything else unraveled?"

"I think she must have done. She's been too good at evading us for too long. Things don't happen coincidentally with that woman."

Berowne, tired of the ribbon game, shook himself, sending the ribbons flying, raced across the room, and jumped onto Mélanie's lap, kneading her mulberry vevlet skirt. Mélanie pressed her face against his fur for a moment. "But even now we know the rest of Lady Shroppington's plan that night, I'm not sure what she wanted in talking to me."

"Some sort of closure, perhaps," Kitty said. "Her whole attempt at revenge seems like an attempt at getting closure on her terms."

"There's no closure in this." Mélanie stroked Berowne's head. "I don't like her, as I admitted. But I can't deny she's like me in many ways."

"I wouldn't say that." Malcolm's voice was neutral and matter-of-fact.

"She combined spying and her romantic life."

Julien gave a short laugh. "Name me one of us who hasn't. Not that I ever admitted to anything approaching romance."

"Where are you, Romeo?" Jessica called out, holding a puppet with long dark hair.

"It's not where, it's wherefore," Colin corrected. *"Wherefore art thou."*

"It means why," Emily added. "Not where."

"Silly Shakespeare," Jessica said. "Mummy, are they right?"

"They are indeed," Mélanie told her daughter. "Many an actress has made a fool of herself reading the line wrong."

"Well, I won't," Jessica declared.

Mélanie grinned at her daughter, then turned to Julien. "The night of the ball, Lady Shroppington admitted your grandfather might have been the love of her life."

Julien set the repaired carriage on the sofa table. "She didn't have very good taste, then. He wasn't a very good spy and he was a rather less good person."

"As Aunt Frances would say, someone's being a good person has very little to do with it," Malcolm said.

"Yes, but Alistair at least was—is—disgustingly clever. My grandfather wasn't."

"He was clever enough to avoid getting caught," Kitty said.

"Until Lady Shroppington," Julien said. "I can see that making him fall in love with her. Though not her falling in love with him."

"Love can be notoriously unpredictable," Raoul said.

The door opened to four enthusiastic children who raced towards the children already in the room. They were the children of Julien's late cousin, Louisa Craven. Behind them were Julien's other cousin, David Mallinson, and David's lover, Simon Tanner, who were now effectively the Craven children's parents. And behind them were—

"Good God," Julien said, as Malcolm and Mélanie got up to greet the new arrivals. "Who invited Uncle Hubert and Aunt Amelia?"

"I did," Mélanie said. "Hubert was a huge help at Emily Cowper's ball. And I did feel we owed Lucinda."

"I asked them to dinner at Mivart's," Raoul added. He had been hosting a Boxing Day dinner at Mivart's since before he was even officially part of the family.

Julien gave a sigh of mock resignation. "It seems there's no escaping my childhood family after all. And do you know, I don't really mind."

MALCOLM MOVED to the table with the mulled wine bowl to refill cups. The library had continued to fill with people. His aunt Frances and her husband Archie, who was Harry's uncle, and their three children. Rupert, Bertrand, Gabrielle, Nick, and young Stephen. Nerezza and Benedict Smythe. And Thomas Thornsby, who had slipped in quietly and was talking to Harry and Cordelia. Edith was with the group on the floor with the children, putting on a puppet show. Like Julien, Malcolm had the memory of a number of lonely childhood Christmases. Raoul was right. The people one spent the holidays with made all the difference.

A flurry of applause announced the end of the puppet show. Lucinda, who had been working the curtain, scrambled up from the carpet and walked over to Malcolm to refill her cup of mulled wine. "This is so fun. I don't remember ever having toys in the library all the time I was growing up."

"I'm glad you're here." Malcolm ladled more mulled wine into her cut-glass cup.

"It's a nice Christmas." Lucinda took a sip of wine. Her gaze went from Edith, still on the floor, to Thomas by the windows with Harry and Cordy. "I do wish Edith and Mr. Thornsby would talk, though."

"So do I," Malcolm said. "But that's something they have to sort out."

Lucinda nodded and frowned into her cup of wine. "I saw Marianne and Charlotte two days ago in the Burlington Arcade. They seemed easier with each other. As though maybe they'd talked. But I don't imagine there's any way things can be easy for them."

Malcolm studied Lucinda. It seemed just yesterday he'd been carrying her on his shoulders or playing on the carpet with her like his own children. "You knew?" he asked.

"Oh, for heaven's sake, Malcolm. I'm not blind. I've known about David and Simon since long before anyone admitted it." Lucinda's gaze went to her brother and Simon, who were both on the floor setting up a new puppet show. "Come to think of it, even now Mama and Papa don't precisely admit it. They simply accept that Simon is part of the family, but they don't put why he is into words." She glanced at her mother, who was talking to Frances, and her father, who was talking to Raoul and Laura. "In any case, if David can love Simon—and if Bertrand and Rupert can love each other, come to think of it—it stands to reason two women could love each other. Marianne and Charlotte have been my best friends this season. And believe me, standing on the edge of the dance floor and lining up at the supper table and going in and out of the retiring room, one spends so much time with the girls in one's season. Not to mention those moments when one escapes to the terrace or an antechamber because one simply has to have a few moments to laugh at the absurdity of it all. I couldn't spend that much time with two people I cared about and not notice."

"Did they talk about it to you?" Malcolm asked. He wasn't sure he'd have worked it out himself if Raoul and Laura hadn't.

"Oh, no. I'm not even sure they talked about it with each other.

I mean, lovers don't always, do they? People can be in love with each other without admitting it to each other."

"Very true," Malcolm said. "I was in love with Mélanie long before I admitted it to myself let alone to her."

"I tried to ask," Lucinda said. "After Marianne got betrothed to Mr. Thornsby. Once I asked her if she really was sure. And when she said, 'Yes, it's what I need to do,' I said, 'But you're in love with someone else.' And she said, 'Don't be silly, Lucy. Whom would I be in love with?' And another time I tried to get Charlotte to talk about it. When she wouldn't, I said, 'How can you simply stand by and let this happen?' And she said, 'It's not my choice to make. And there's not really any other path for Marianne to be happy besides being a wife.' I said that was absurd, hadn't she read Juliette Dubretton and Mary Woll-stonecraft? And she said that had nothing to do with the lives we lived in Mayfair. I said that was silly, we could always walk away from Mayfair. And she said that was far easier to say than to do, and one would never ask someone one loved to do that. That's the closest she came to admitting she loved Marianne. It was fairly close, now I think of it." Lucinda studied Malcolm for a long moment. "Did you know? About David and Simon? Right away?"

"I could tell something was possible the night they met. But I'd known David a lot longer than you'd known Marianne and Charlotte."

"And you knew about David?"

Malcolm hesitated. He tried to be honest about such things with his own children. And Lucinda deserved an honest answer. If he could manage to frame one. "Your brother and I had been close friends since we were at school."

"So he confided in you?"

"Not in so many words." Malcolm saw David's face in that moment he'd seen David looking at another boy and then met David's gaze, and the silent acknowledgment that had passed between them. "We never discussed it. But I knew. And David knew I knew.."

"So it's like with David and my parents."

Malcolm bit back a retort at the idea that his response to David was anything like that of Hubert and Amelia, who had put David through so much. "Not precisely. As I said, David knew what I was aware of."

"Well, I think now he knows that our parents know. I mean, he'd be an idiot not to. And David's not an idiot. He's the opposite. But you never tried to make David be someone he isn't. And you actually talk to him about it now, don't you?"

"Well, yes." Malcolm glanced at Simon, arranging puppet theatre scenery, and David, helping their adopted daughter Amy costume a doll. It was accepted in their circle that David and Simon were a couple. Did they talk to them openly about being a couple? Malcolm scoured his memory of recent conversations. Of course it was always implied. It was understood by all of them. David still tended not to put it into words. Simon did. Had Malcolm ever done so himself? Suddenly the thought that he might not have done so bothered him intensely.

"I mean, you should be able to talk about it with your friends," Lucinda said. "You talk about being married to Mélanie with your friends, don't you?"

"I don't talk about anything personal easily. But yes."

Lucinda nodded. "I hope Marianne and Charlotte can at least talk about it with each other. I mean, I've not been in love with anyone, but I'd think that's the minimum?"

Malcolm lifted his cup of wine to her own. "I couldn't agree more."

"You must despise me," Thomas said in a low voice.

"Thomas!" Edith started and nearly spilled the cup of mulled wine she had picked up before she went to talk to him at last, knowing she would need fortification. "No. How could I?"

He gave a wry smile. "I haven't made the best choices."

"How can one know if a choice is right until one sees how it plays out?" She gulped down a sip of wine and set the cup on a pier table before she downed the entire contents. It wouldn't help to be lightheaded. "You weren't exactly dealing with easy options."

"Damn it." Thomas lunged away from the bookcase he was leaning against, took two steps forwards, checked himself, then moved the rest of the way to her and seized her hands, heedless of the others in the room. "The only thing that makes sense in this madness is us. And we've risked losing it. Marry me, Edith."

Shock coursed through her. And something else. A giddy rush that might have been happiness. "Thomas. None of this changes anything."

"Doesn't it? We've tried to be practical. *I've* tried to be practical. You've been kind and not hated me for it. And all that happened is more people's lives were almost upended."

"That's because—"

"Don't say it's because of Marianne. No one deserves a bloodless marriage. If there's one thing that's clear to me in this mess it's that I don't want to lose you, Edith." He drew back and scanned her face. "I fully realize you may not feel the same."

"It's not—how I feel doesn't matter."

"For god's sake, Edith. You must know how you feel matters more than anything."

"Nothing's changed for your family."

"I'm not going to secure their happiness by denying our own. Let me worry about my family. The only question is what you want. I know you aren't sure you want to marry. And I know even if you decide you do want to marry, I don't have a great deal to offer. To put it mildly."

"Thomas. For god's sake. You were just saying marriage shouldn't be bloodless. You're quite right that I don't want to marry. Not in general. It seems far too fraught with risks. The only thing that would tempt me to it is marrying *you*."

Something sparked in Thomas's eyes. "You mean—"

Edith returned the clasp of his hands and tossed caution to the wind. "Yes."

❧

"All in all, a happier Christmas than I expected." Mélanie unclasped the garnet earrings Malcolm had given her for Christmas. "Certainly happier than it seemed it would be ten days ago."

"It's always a risk," Malcolm said.

"Marriage?" She met his gaze through the flickering candlelight in the looking glass.

"Among other things. But yes. I'm glad Thomas and Edith were willing to take the risk."

Mélanie set the earrings in their velvet-lined box. "Even though we were worrying about where it might lead little more than a week ago?"

"Oh, I'm still worried." Malcolm shrugged off his coat. "The more one cares, the more things can go horribly wrong. But then, love's always a risk. I spent too much of my life not taking risks. It's a bleak alternative."

In the looking glass, Malcolm's gaze was uncharacteristically dark. Mélanie turned round to look at him directly. "Even more of a risk for Marianne Schofield and Charlotte Wilcox. Assuming they're willing to take it."

Malcolm nodded. "Lucinda talked to me. Before we went to Mivart's. She'd known about Marianne and Charlotte for weeks."

"That makes sense. I knew she was holding something back. Marianne confided in her? Or Charlotte?"

"No, Lucinda pieced it together." Malcolm draped his coat over the back of the green velvet armchair and smoothed the black cassimere. "She asked me about David. When I knew about David.

And then she asked if we talked to David and Simon about their relationship."

"We do. That is—"

"You talk to Simon."

"Well, yes. You and David don't talk much about relationships in general. But we all know—"

"We know, but it's all implied. I suddenly found myself feeling wrong for not putting it into words."

"I'm not sure we put it into words that Kitty and Julien are married. We were all at their wedding."

"Which David and Simon can't have."

"Which is damnable. But I'm not sure David would thank us for putting into words something he's still reticent to put into words himself."

"I don't want to be like Hubert."

"You couldn't be like Hubert if you tried, darling. But if you mean we may not always recognize that our friends have challenges we don't—it's a fair point. In the happy little bubble of the people we were with tonight, it's easy to forget that they have to lie about who they are every day." The words stuck in her throat. "It makes being a former Bonapartist spy seem positively easy."

Malcolm grinned and crossed to her side. "Two years ago, we didn't think we'd ever be able to come back to Britain."

"Three years ago, I didn't think you'd ever trust me again." She got up from her dressing table bench to stand beside him. "Of course, perhaps I'm delusional and you don't. You are a very good agent."

He slid his arms round her. "Don't talk rot, sweetheart."

"That's my Malcolm. Always ready with a romantic turn of phrase."

He bent his head and kissed her. "Happy Christmas, Mel."

She wrapped her arms round his neck and returned the kiss. Sometimes conventional phrases one had once thought one would never use said everything. "Happy Christmas, darling."

THE SEVEN DIALS AFFAIR

Malcolm and Mélanie Suzanne Rannoch's adventures in espionage and investigation continue in Tracy Grant's new historical mystery
On sale May 2023

Prologue

Buenos Aires
1818

Kitty Ashford tightened her fingers on the folds of her cloak. The wind tugged the hood back and the moon was bright enough that her hair might catch the light. Red blonde was not the most convenient color for a spy.

The wind brought the scent of the water from the docks, mixed with tar and grease and sour ale. She scanned the dark line of buildings. He was there, leaning against the side of a shed, blurring into the shadows. Somehow even the lines of his body echoed the lines of the wood. She'd never fail to marvel at his skill. And at other things.

He turned as she approached and took a step forwards, as though unfolding from the shadows. She saw the quick gleam of his smile and an echoing flash in his eyes.

"I'm sorry," he said, when she was close enough for speech to be safe. "I'm sure it wasn't convenient to get away."

"I'm used to it." She'd had to make an excuse to her husband, but this far into her marriage that was hardly novel. "But I assume it's important?"

"I'm afraid so." The light shifted, as the wind set the clouds ruffling over the moon. Something leapt in his eyes. "I'm going to have to leave. Tonight."

Her muscles jerked. Like she'd received a blow to the gut. Stupid. She'd known this was coming at some point. Why be shocked it was now? "We were right about the leak?"

"Yes. I need to get back with the news. I can't trust it to someone else."

"Of course. The only reason you were here was to find a safe place to hide. And now it isn't safe anymore."

"That isn't the only reason I was here. Or at least not the only reason I stayed here."

"Don't, Julien." She took a step back "Your saving grace has always been that you didn't pretend we were anything we weren't or give way to platitudes."

"That wasn't either of those." He took her hand, his fingers steady. "Lie low for a bit. We don't know how much got out and how far it's gone."

She nodded. "I'll be all right. I've been through this in Spain. It comes with the territory."

His fingers tightened over her own. "Tell the boys goodbye. I'd have liked to see them."

Her sons were fond of Julien, despite not knowing his true name. In fact both Leo and Timothy were rather alarmingly good at seeing through his disguises. "They'll understand. They're both used to changes."

"I'll find a way to write. And we both don't know where we may end up."

"Julien. Don't pretend this is something it isn't."

"I'm not pretending anything, Kitkat." He released her hand, but only to pull her into his arms and put his mouth to hers.

For a moment, the world rushed away. As much as it ever could for them. She slid her arms round him, holding him tight. Perhaps too tight. When he released her, she was breathless. "For once I don't think you had half a mind to who might sneak up behind us."

"With you I'm always inclined to lose my head."

"Liar." She kept her hands at her sides. She was not going to give way to the cliché impulse to touch her hand to her abdomen. She wasn't even sure. And even if she hadn't been it didn't, couldn't concern him.

He bent his head to kiss her again. How provoking of Julien, who was so expert at lying about everything, to be so damnably honest when he kissed.

"Stay safe, Kitkat."

"My dear. Don't ask the impossible."

Their gazes caught for a moment. "Do you know where the leak came from?" she asked.

"Nothing conclusive. But I suspect we were right in our suspicions. Which makes things all the more complicated."

"Have a care, Julien. It's a dangerous time for you to go back."

"It's dangerous to be alive. But somehow I've managed for close to four decades." He took her hand and lifted it to his lips. "I'm sure we'll meet again. I only hope we're on the same side."

She stepped back and drew her cloak round her like armour. "Oh, Julien. What did I say about to asking the impossible?"

Chapter One

Seven Dials, London

Malcolm Rannoch slipped through the shadowy crowd. Over a decade of training as a spy told him not to stand out, but there was a limit to what one could do in gentleman's garb in Seven Dials. If he'd had more time he'd have donned a disguise, but the summons had been urgent. And his wife was at the theatre and not there to help him.

He skirted a steaming mess that looked to have been dumped from a chamber pot, ducked round two men who had come to fisticuffs, and turned the corner in the warren of sixteenth-century streets. Only a few streets away from the the Tavistock Theatre where his wife was yet a world away. Fewer surprised gazes turned in his direction than he'd have expected. But then he'd passed more than a few men in silk hats and well-cut coats. *Don't be silly, darling.* He could hear his wife's voice in his ear. *Anyone who sees you will just think you're on your way to a brothel. Dozens of men from Mayfair are doing the same tonight.*

He turned up the collar of his coat, aware of the heat in his cheeks. Idiot, not to have thought of the obvious excuse. And to be discomfited by it. Too many years of civilian life were turning him soft. Not that there was anything particularly civilian about scarcely going two months without demands from a former spymaster. One of whom happened to be his father and his wife's spymaster. The other of whom had been his own spymaster and was far more lethal.

A sailor's shanty cut the air, interlaced with a version of *Over the Hills and Far Away* from a street over. He paused, and the inn sign of three ladies in gold crowns caught his eye through the greasy lamplight. He climbed the steps and pushed open the door of the Three Queens. Heads turned in his direction. It was easier, he realized, when he had Mélanie with him. For one thing everyone looked at her. And no one questioned what he was about when he had a woman on his arm. Which was disturbing in and of itself but also useful.

But Mélanie was at the Tavistock rehearsing her new play, and he was on this mission alone. Which happened more and more of late.

He pushed his way between the splintery tables, over the ale-soaked floorboards, with a careless ease he'd have never felt in a tavern in his own persona. *Of course, dearest.* Again he could hear his wife's voice. *Life is so much easier when one is playing a role. Why do you think I played one for so long? Why do you think I still do?*

The play's the thing. He knew the barkeep was looking at him, but he didn't stop to make eye contact. His summons had been quite clear on where he should go.

A red-haired woman in a clinging green gown brushed against him as he moved to the stairs. "I'm available, guv'nor."

"Sorry." Malcolm paused and smiled at her. "I have business to see to."

He climbed the stairs, aware of more gazes on him. Though not surprised gazes. They assumed, like the disappointed woman in the green dress, that he was on his way upstairs to visit one of the women who worked the tavern. Who a decade or so ago might have been the remarkable woman who was now his wife. Which somehow made the thought of being taken for that man more discomfiting. He wasn't sure whether to be grateful or not that Mélanie wasn't with him.

At the top of the stairs, he went to the door his note had indicated, the third one. He rapped once, then opened it without waiting for a response.

The smell swamped him at once. Sweet, cloying.

A woman was stretched out on the floorboards, fair hair spread round her, the pale folds of her gown and black velvet of her cloak tangled round her legs, as though she had fallen in a sudden tumble.

A man was bending over her. Tall, wrapped in a loose greatcoat, brown hair ruffled. That was not surprising either. Jeremy Roth had summoned Malcolm, and Malcolm had been quite sure when he received the cryptic missive that it was because of an investigation, probably a murder. Roth was a skilled Bow Street runner, but he was quick to employ Malcolm and his friends' assistance when it suited a case.

Malcolm pushed the door to as Roth's head jerked up from contemplation of the victim. "Mel's at the Tavistock. But I came as soon as I could."

"Thank you." Roth's voice was unusually husky, his gaze opaque in the greasy light of the tallow candle on the gateleg table by the window.

Malcolm moved forwards. A spreading red stain showed on the woman's chest through the white muslin of her gown. The blood had congealed. Her eyes were glazed. He didn't need to feel for a pulse to know she was dead. "How long do you think?" he asked Roth.

"An hour perhaps. Not much more."

Malcolm had spent enough hours cooling his heels at his wife's modiste's to recognize the quality of the muslin and velvet, the elegance of the cut of the clothes. And her earrings and necklace had the gleam of real gold despite the poor light. "She doesn't look like a woman one would expect to find in Seven Dials." Which would explain why Roth had summoned him. He often wanted Malcolm and Mélanie's and their friends' assistance with cases involving the beau monde. "You'd like us to assist on the case?"

"No," Roth said. His gaze jerked to Malcolm's own. His hands were lose at his sides. He wasn't, Malcolm realized, holding his notebook, which was usually ever-present in investigations. "That is, your assistance would be invaluable. But I won't be able to oversee this case myself."

Malcolm took another step forwards. The Bow Street Public Office was under the auspices of the home office, which meant cases that involved anything to do with the government, espionage, or the royal family were particularly fraught. He didn't recognize the woman as someone connected to the government or royal family or as an agent, but he might not know. "Why not?"

Roth looked down at the dead woman again, But though his gaze was fixed on her tangled limbs and still features, for a moment it was as though he was looking not at her in the present but into some hell of his own making. "Because this is my wife."

Malcolm stared at his friend. He had first met Roth in the Peninsula, during the war against Napoleon Bonaparte's forces, when Roth had been a soldier assigned to intelligence missions and Malcolm a diplomatic attaché and agent. They hadn't talked much about their personal lives, but Roth had mentioned a wife at home and children. Later when Malcolm, settled in London as an MP and seemingly free of the intelligence game (which now seemed a joke), had encountered Roth again as a Bow Street runner, Roth had referred to his wife as "gone." He hadn't offered further details and Malcolm hadn't felt the right to pry for them. He knew Roth lived with his his sister, who was helping him raise his two sons. Despite Roth's reticence about the beau monde, they had all frequently been guests in Malcolm and Mélanie's home.

"I didn't know she was back in England," Malcolm said.

Roth met Malcolm's gaze, his own suddenly focused. "And you're wondering if I found her like this or if she was alive when I came into the room."

Once Malcolm had confronted a similar question about a dead woman he had been found bending over. The person who had found him was his wife Mélanie. And the dead woman was a lady many—including his wife—assumed to be his mistress, though in fact she was his half-sister. He still remembered the doubt in

Mélanie's eyes, how it had cut him in two, and how he had known he had no right to question her questions.

"I'd never ask that of a friend."

"But as an investigator you're too good not to ask that of a suspect. Which is what I am."

"For God's sake, Jeremy." Malcolm caught Roth's arm. "Before everything else, my deepest sympathies."

Roth stared up at him, eyes glazed with confusion.

"Your wife just died." Malcolm pressed Roth into a chair. He looked round. There was a bottle of wine on the gateleg table, but he didn't want to disturb anything. Not yet. He strode out the door, called for a glass of gin, brought it back and put it in Roth's hand.

Roth took a gulp and spoke quickly. "I hadn't heard from Allegra in years. Not since she left. Then I received a note from her this evening, not two hours since, asking me to come here and meet her. I would have thought it was a set-up save that I'd know her hand anywhere. I found her like this. She was beyond help, though I did everything I could for her." His voice caught. He took another swallow of gin and pushed on. "I realize how improbable that sounds."

"Far too improbable to be anything a man with your skills would have invented," Malcolm said.

"That's one way of looking at it." Roth stared down into the glass. "Allegra never seemed satisfied. Our life wasn't easy. I knew it wasn't the life she had dreamed of. She could get caught up in moments of fun with the boys, but a part of me always knew she was dissatisfied. Shocking as it was that she disappeared, a part of me wasn't surprised. After all, what else is a woman to do when she's unhappy with her life? Divorce was far out of our reach."

"Did she leave a note?"

Roth shook his head. He was determinedly not looking away from his wife's body. "She went out to do some shopping one afternoon and never returned. I scoured the streets. I used every source I could find. Shamelessly. I'd have asked you for help if we'd been better friends then."

"I'm sorry we weren't."

"I was able to trace her as far as the Red Lion on the Dover Road. I couldn't find anyone who'd actually seen her on the stage. I had a vague description that might mean she'd got into a private carriage. And another vague description in an inn at Dover."

"She never wrote?"

"Not until today."

"Do you have reason to think she went off with a lover?"

"It seems an obvious assumption," Roth said, as though discussing a victim to whom he had no connection. "I had no evidence she had a lover before she left. Except the growing distance between us. And her increasing absences."

Malcolm looked down at Allegra Roth's body. He noted again the lines of her gown and cloak, the gleam of her jewelry. "A fashionable modiste made this gown. And that's real gold."

"Yes. All far finer than anything she had when she was married to me." Roth's eyes narrowed, the gaze of an investigator. "I can't imagine she was staying here."

"Have you questioned the tavern staff?"

"Briefly, when I paid the pot boy to bring you the letter. I didn't want to rouse their suspicions, but apparently Allegra arrived veiled and engaged a private room. They made the obvious assumptions about why she was expecting a gentleman. She wasn't dressed for Seven Dials, but I doubt she's the only fashionable lady to engage a private room here." Roth got to his feet but didn't move closer to his wife's body. "She was stabbed. One cut, expertly done or a lucky hit. No sign of the weapon."

Malcolm looked round. "Did you—?"

"Search? Yes. So there's no way to prove I didn't take anything. But you'd best look as well in case I missed anything."

A reticule lay beside her, velvet with a steel clasp, like many Mélanie had. An enamel tin of lip rouge, a crystal atomizer of scent, a light gardenia. A silk coin purse. An ivory comb. A stray button.

"Does any of this mean anything to you?" Malcolm asked.

"Only the button. It's from our eldest son's first shirt. I didn't even know she'd taken it. It makes me wonder—" His face twisted. "I'm going to have to send for Bow Street. They'll turn the investigation over to someone and keep me out of it. I may well be arrested, if not tonight, then soon. No." He put up a hand as Malcolm started to protest. "You know a husband or wife would be the first suspect, especially if they're found with the body. It won't play well that I summoned you first, but that's why I had to. I need you to promise you'll look into this. Whatever you can learn. I know I may be putting you against the home office—"

"Hardly for the first time."

Roth's gaze locked on his own. "I know what I'm asking."

"You can't imagine I wouldn't help."

"No." Roth held his gaze for a long moment that spoke volumes about where their friendship had come. He reached in his greatcoat pocket and pulled out two pieces of paper torn from his notebook. "If I'm arrested before I can go home this is for Harriet. And this is for the boys."

Malcolm took the papers. "Mélanie once found me over the dead body of the woman she believed to be my mistress. She helped me in the investigation."

"Did she suspect you?"

"She tried not to let me see it."

"You're doing a good job of that yourself."

Malcolm looked levelly into Roth's gaze. "One can never be sure of what anyone might do. But I know you. Better perhaps than Mélanie knew me at that time. I can't imagine your doing this."

"That may be a failure of your imagination."

"Always possible. But I choose to think otherwise."

"You need to keep an open mind. Because more than anything,

I want to know what happened. Allegra deserves that. My sons need to know what happened to their mother. Promise you'll learn the truth, Malcolm. Wherever it takes you."

Malcolm looked into the eyes of the man who was one of his closest friends, for all the secrets on both sides. "I promise."

MIDWINTER INTRIGUE

THE DUKE'S GAMBIT

SECRETS OF A LADY

THE MASK OF NIGHT

THE DARLINGTON LETTERS

THE GLENISTER PAPERS

A MIDWINTER'S MASQUERADE

THE TAVISTOCK PLOT

THE CARFAX INTRIGUE

THE WESTMINSTER INTRIGUE

THE APSLEY HOUSE INCIDENT

THE WHITEHALL CONSPIRACY

Forthcoming May 2023—THE SEVEN DIALS AFFAIR

ACKNOWLEDGMENTS

Every book in this series starts with a huge thanks to the amazing team at Nancy Yost Literary Agency who help bring the series to life. To my fabulous agent, Nancy Yost, for her insights from the start of the series, her steadfast support, and her brilliant eye for editing cover copy. To Natanya Wheeler for her keen insights, for once again shepherding the book expertly through the publication process and getting it out into the world, and creating another fabulous cover that brings to life both Mélanie Rannoch and the holiday ball that is the setting for the story. To Sarah Younger for superlative social media support and for helping the book along through production and publication. To Fiona O'Flynn for a great set of quote cards. And to the entire team at Nancy Yost Literary Agency for their fabulous work. Their creativity and dedication make all of them a dream to work with. Malcolm, Mélanie, and I are all very fortunate to have their support.

Thank you to Eve Lynch for the meticulous and thoughtful copyediting. I love sharing the Rannochs with you and so appreciate your care for getting their story right when it comes to everything from historical usage to series continuity. Already excited for our next collaboration.

Thank you to Kristen Loken for a magical new author photo taken on one of my and my daughter Mélanie's favorite occasions of the year, the Merola Grand Finale. We are so excited to have had this event again this year, and it was great moment to capture a new photo. Your brilliance never fails to amaze me, Kristen!

I am very fortunate to have a wonderful group of writer

friends near and far who make being a writer less solitary. Thanks in particular to Lauren Willig for sharing the joys of historical research and the challenges of juggling life as a writer and a mom. To Penelope Williamson, for sharing adventures, analyzing plots from Shakespeare to *Scandal*, and being a wonderful honorary aunt to my daughter. So glad we are able to travel together again. Thank you to the #momswritersclub on Twitter for bimonthly chats that are energizing and inspiring, and especially to Jessica Payne for starting it and to Jessica and Sara Read for their wonderful #MomsWritersClub YouTube channel on which Mélanie and I had the fun of doing a guest interview, and for fabulous Zoom writing sprints—during one of which much of the teaser to *The Seven Dials Affair* was written.

Thank you to the readers who support Malcolm and Mélanie and their friends and provide wonderful insights on my Web site and social media, and especially on the Goodreads Discussion Group for the series.

Thanks to Gregory Paris and jim saliba for creating and updating a fabulous website that chronicles Malcolm and Mélanie's adventures.

And thank you to my daughter Mélanie, who helped me brainstorm *The Mayfair Mistletoe Plot*, came up with one of the major plot twists, suggested some perfect details for the epilogue, and proofread. You were an amazing support, sweetheart, and I am so proud that my website now includes "Mélanie's Corner" for your stories, starting with your wonderful series *Talea's Mysteries*.

From the time she could touch the keys, Mélanie has contributed something to each of my books. This is Mélanie's contribution to this story –"I could not be prouder of Mummy for the amazing stories she writes! I am so happy I got to help with this book! But am even happier to be the daughter of such an amazing writer, person, and mummy! I was inspired to start writing because of my mummy, and I get inspiration for my stories from Mummy!"

ABOUT THE AUTHOR

Photo by Kristen Loken, https:// kristenloken.com

Tracy Grant studied British history at Stanford University and received the Firestone Award for Excellence in Research for her honors thesis on shifting conceptions of honor in late-fifteenth-century England. She lives in the San Francisco Bay Area with her young daughter and four cats. In addition to writing, Tracy works for the Merola Opera Program, a professional training program for opera singers, pianists, and stage directors. Her real-life heroine is her daughter Mélanie, who is very cooperative about Mummy's writing time and is starting to write herself. She is currently at work on her next book chronicling the adventures of Malcolm and Mélanie Suzanne Rannoch. Visit her on the web at www.tracygrant.org.